STORM SWIFT AND THE SEVENTH KEY

An Adventure Story

Stephanie de Winter

Stephanie de Winter

ISBN: 9798579444103

Cover design by: Heather Innes
Library of Congress Control Number: 2018675309
Printed in the United States of America

STORM SWIFT AND THE SEVENTH KEY

Puffin Island is home to Storm Swift. Her dark anxious world is transformed after she is suspended from school. From Hell School to Home School, Storm flourishes. Finn, her cousin, arrives on the island one stormy night after running away from his psychopathic step dad, and together they discover the mysterious underworld of the island that contains tunnels, secrets, puzzles to be solved, and a shipwreck.

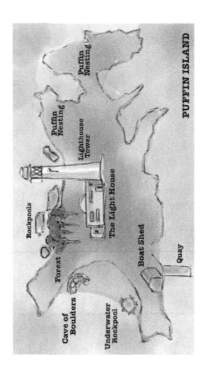

CHAPTER 1
The Plan

Storm Swift, sat in her round bedroom high up in the lighthouse tower, glaring at the homework given by "call me Tess" the anxiety counsellor. Task one: to describe her feelings that day in a "Feelings Journal." Her mum and Grandad Flint thought this was a great idea. Task two: include a feelings scale from one to ten. One equals angry, and ten equals happy. The other numbers were feelings in between. Like ten was ever gonna be used!

"It will be a private journal Storm. Helps to get your thoughts and feelings down on paper." Tess said, explaining that it was "cathartic" which means, "relief through expressing strong emotions."

Storm was now in a state of desperation. Her anxiety issues were ruining her life, preventing her from going to school or, sleepovers. Even her home life was laced with a constant sick feeling. But she also felt angry, frustrated and exhausted by the constant battle raging within her. Lately, her stress levels were so high it was a struggle to concentrate even on the smallest task. Concentration scale: zero point five out of ten!

Her mum, Lily Swift, had taken her to Smith's newsagents to buy a journal.

"What about a nice cheerful one?" Her mum optimistically held up a pink one with cup cakes on the cover. Storm had shaken her head scornfully. No way!

"This is cool." Storm picked up a black journal with white skulls printed on it. Black was her favourite colour. Pink? Really!

So far she'd managed to fill in the personal details section of the journal but she doubted the journal was going to see a whole lot of attention.

Name: Storm Avie Swift

Parents: Flint and Lily Swift

Initials: S A S which is cool as my dad's a Captain in the SAS which is military: Special Forces.

Age: Fourteen.

Hair: Long blonde, but soon to be dark green!

Eye Colour: Olive

Appearance: Pretty & Athletic (My friend Jenny said to put.)

Activities & Interests: Rock music. Swimming. All animals, nature and reading

Intellect: Pretty smart (Holly my other bf said to put).

Height: Five foot five inches.

Physical Health: Awesome.

Mental Health: Beyond Tragic!

School: Shelley High School (should be renamed: Shelley Hell School)

Attendance: Three days out of thirty days this month. At least I managed three! No one seems to get that!

Address:

The Light House Tower

The Light House

Puffin Island

Shelley

Feeling Scale:- minus ten and angry! Hate everyone! Sick of feeling sad and anxious.

I officially hate school. Miss Pinch, the school nurse, is a fake. I don't trust her. Understanding scale - equals zero! Obviously they (teachers) all think my school anxiety is bs, and I'm making it up. Mum gets it but they're just horrible to her. Mum says it's because we've mucked up their attendance figures on some Ofsted report. Why would I make it up? Just what every kid my age wants! To sit in the Cube (School quiet room) and be judged! (That's sarcasm!). If I had smashed up my leg, like Grandad Flint, they'd be doing everything possible to help me. My mind is broken and everyone judges me and thinks it's bs.

Mum's panicking about social workers. I feel sick and dizzy all the time at school. It's like cold fingernails clawing at my stomach and a feeling of dread times one hundred. Tomorrow, after being tortured in hell (School), I'm gonna dye my hair dark green like seaweed. The school will go mental. In truth I'm totally done. Major depression! Just need to be homeschooled. I have no other solution.

CHAPTER 2
Shelley Hell School

Storm could hear her mother's voice, full of anxiety calling up the spiral staircase to her bedroom at the top of the lighthouse tower.

"Storm, it's nearly eight o'clock! You'll be late for school."

Storm hid under the covers, her stomach rotating like a washing machine on a slow cycle. Her ginger cat Marmalade was sitting on her shoulder, sympathetically kneading her.

"I don't feel well Mum." She mumbled, clinging onto the bed sheet for dear life. The thought of spending another day at school made her feel like her whole life was crumbling to dust, and suffocating her. Her heart thudded in her chest.

"Can't you just try to go?" Her mother pleaded, appearing in the arched doorway like a hazy apparition through the thin cotton of the sheet. She sat down on the edge of the bed.

"I can't." Storm began to cry.

"I know it's hard for you but I'm worried we'll get into trouble with the school and social services. We agreed, you'd go in at least two days a week. You're such a clever girl. You need an education. It's important."

Storm huddled further into the warmth and safety of her bed. No one seemed to understand. If they did, why would they keep pressurising her to attend? It was pure torture.

"Please Storm, just try!"

Arriving late for registration, Storm fought nausea, terrified she was going to be sick in front of her class-mates. Wobbling up to Miss Young, pale faced and tearful, she appealed, to be allowed to go home sick.

"I really don't feel well. I think I have a sickness and diarrhoea bug." Storm knew that anyone with a stomach upset was guaranteed at least two days off school.

Ms Young's eyebrows shot upwards unbecomingly.

"Again?" Pursing her lips she appraised her. "You'll have to go to the nurse's office and see Miss Pinch."

"Please can't I just go home? I might spread it."

Ms Young shook her head disapprovingly. She wasn't convinced, and pointed in the direction of the nurse's office.

"What's the matter this time?" Nurse Pinch asked sternly, narrowing her eyes suspiciously. She clearly thought Storm was making it up. "You can talk to me. It's private." A false smile, through yellow gritted teeth. The smile didn't reach her eyes and looked more like a grimace.

"Don't feel well. Light headed an' I feel sick."

"Have you been sick?" demanded Nurse Pinch.

"No."

"How long have you had these symptoms?"

"Yesterday an' today. It's only when I'm here. I'm alright at home." Why wouldn't they just send her home?

"You've problems at home?" The nurse asked briskly, in response.

Storm looked at her in confusion. The nurse wasn't listening properly.

"No. School. Feel ill here." Her head felt dizzy and foggy even talking was an effort. Storm felt detached from her surroundings, as if she was dreaming and wasn't really there.

The nurse tut-tutted, making notes on her clip-board. Dropping her biro, it clattered to the floor. The mere tap tapping of the pen hitting the tiles was magnified as if the volume in Storm's ears had been turned to full.

"We'll contact your mother and your family liaison officer. You must have one?"

Storm looked at her blankly.

"Must I?"

Miss Pinch continued on her stream of contacts:

"Mrs Temple, our new head teacher, will need to be informed, as this is not an isolated incident, and your registration teacher Ms Young. You can spend the rest of the day in the Cube. "

Storm looked at her in horror. The Cube was the quiet classroom where kids with problems were sent! Everyone would know! And so much for the private conversation. She might as well have announced it over the school Tannoy system or put it on Shelley News and Views Facebook page.

Storm brushed back blonde damp hair from her clammy forehead.

"School's important to get an education." The nurse said briskly. "Your mother should have told you that." She clicked her tongue disapprovingly at the mention of her mother, which Storm thought was unfair as her mother did everything possible to encourage her to go to school.

Staring at Nurse Pinch's ugly, tight pointed face, with mean dark eyes like shrivelled currents, Storm felt anger uncurling from the pit of her belly.

"She tells me every day. It's not her fault!" Storm glared at her.

Storm was desperate. In her mind all she could see was Puffin Island and her warm friendly round bedroom and cats Marmalade and Marmite. The island with its caves, rockpools, puffins and gulls was her sanctuary. The school was loud, cold and terrifying. It made her feel ill and she didn't know why.

Her anxiety was crippling. Storm knew logically that school was in fact a safe place to be, but try telling her body that. It seemed to think she'd been dropped into a warzone.

The nurse ordered her out of sick bay into the chaos of the noisy corridors packed full of a stream of chattering, laughing children swarming their way to the cafeteria for break, or , down the hill to the chip shop and bakery situated in the High Street. The noise was deafening and echoed through her skull. It was embarrassing enough having the awful Nurse Pinch prodding her in the back. She bit her lip, trying not to cry. How she hated the satanic nurse.

The school acted as if she was a deviant, trying to play truant and be disruptive. What they failed to understand was that this couldn't be further from the truth. All she wanted was to attend school daily, experience zero anxiety, and be happy like the other pupils at school, but her body wouldn't let her. Instead of helping her, it was as if she was being punished for something that seemed to be out of her control.

The afternoon seemed to go on for an eternity as she sat in the Cube cringing, praying that no one passing would see her through the open door. She'd been given a book to read that she'd read back in junior school. The teachers were all talking to her softly and slowly, as if she were six and didn't understand words.

The school bell jangled, declaring the end of the school day. Like a race horse waiting to be released from the stalls, she shot out of the building tearing down the hill to the High Street. Storm was on her way to the chemist.

CHAPTER 3
Seaweed Hair

"Storm!"

Her friend's voice carried through the sound of rock music. Pulling air pods out of her ears, she turned to see her friend Jenny, whom she'd known since primary school, running down the hill after her.

"Hi Jen. I'm just popping to the shop then home."

"I'll walk with you. Didn't see you in maths?"

"Same old …"

"Aw. I was hoping things were cool now."

"Naw, Old Pinch sent me to the Cube! Mum's stressed out. School giving her a hard time."

"That sucks! You think they'd help. Any news on your dad?"

"He's on exercise somewhere up north. Shetland I think. You'll have to come over. You know we moved in with my grandad a couple of weeks ago? I'm sorry I haven't texted. Just been trying to sort stuff out."

"We're cool. Always, Storm you know that, but text me next time you feel bad. And living on Puffin Island! Everyone knows! You're like famous! Small town and all. Is your grandad okay now?"

"Yeah just a broken ankle. He slipped on the rocks clearing tree mallow, but it made sense for us to move in as we spent so much time there anyway and with Dad being away so much."

"We'll have to go exploring. Is the tree mallow still a problem?"

"Yeah it's like a big weed just spreads and stops the puffins nesting."

"Happy to come over and help do some weeding."

"Aw thanks Jen. It's kinda my job for now so that would be cool."

"Be fun."

"It's awesome there. You'll love it. It's only a five minute boat ride."

"I'd love to come over. Text you later Storm."

The girls hugged.

Storm entered the chemist, skulking around the bargain trolley full of reduced price products. Dark emerald hair dye looked back at her - price slashed to fifty pence for clearance! She smiled. Just what she was after. She had thick long blonde hair so this could work. The registration teacher's words hovered in the air above the hair products.

'Let me remind you that our strict uniform code is to be adhered to. Makeup and dyed hair are strictly forbidden! Skirts are to be worn just above the knee NOT just below one's bottom! Anyone failing to comply will and I say, WILL, be suspended indefinitely!'

The teacher had given her a 'get out of jail free card'.

Anxious exhaustion may-be hampering her judgment, shunning sense and hugging relief from the problem, but the truth was that Storm simply couldn't face another school day like the hell she'd been through that day. Picking up three cardboard boxes of hair dye, she felt guilty. Her poor mother would go mental.

Catching sight of herself in the thin makeup mirror, her reflection hid her inner turmoil well. Storm resembled her mother, with big olive eyes, a small nose and nice white even teeth. She sighed. What choice did she have? Her mental health issues were a curse that consumed and tarnished her entire world.

Storm saw a counsellor once a month and it was helpful to vent her anger. She'd tried hypnosis, which was like being sent into a deep daydream. It was relaxing but a bit hippy and made her giggle. Fitness training for anxiety she loved. It included yoga, boxing, swimming and running.

Unfortunately, the results were short-lived as she felt great until she returned to school. Then anxiety swooped, enveloping her in its freezing, dark, churning fog once more.

Desperation called for drastic measures. Storm was fading and had to save herself. Hence the idea of dying her hair. Storm paid for the items, stuffing them into her backpack. Texting her mum, she let her know that she was going to walk the two miles back to Puffin Island and she'd text her from the quayside to be picked up by motorboat.

CHAPTER 4
Puffin Island

Walking along the pavement, Storm could see the white lighthouse on Puffin Island glinting in the distant sunlight. Turning down the road that led to the beach, her legs were tickled by the long grasses. Red poppies danced in the breeze, and butterflies of orange and yellow zoomed through the air at speed, as if racing her back to the island. Reaching the end of the road, she walked through a parking area, then down a private track that led to the white fluffy sand and the boat house and quay.

Puffin Island had belonged to the Swift family for centuries. About twenty years ago her grandad, Flint Swift, invented a very successful software programme and made a lot of money. He'd invested the money by converting and extending the lighthouse dwelling attached to the main lighthouse tower and lamp, calling it "The Light House".

The interior of the building was spacious and elegant, with reinforced glass walls on one side, overlooking the ocean all the way to Fife. The roof had been renovated and a stained glass dome inserted in the centre of the house. This brought fragments of colourful light dancing into the building. The name, The Light House, had a double meaning. One, that it was bright and full of light, and the other referred to the actual lighthouse itself. The house consisted of many floors, with nooks and crannies, including a vast cellar on two levels where her grandad stored wine in a massive honeycomb wine rack, alongside other groceries and household items.

The island was volcanic, hilly and approximately a mile and a half long and wide. The lighthouse lamp was still in operation but now automated. Storm shared the home with her mother, Grandad Flint, two cats, and her father, when he was home, which was not often as he was military, Special Forces. "He's away keeping us safe," her mother often said, looking out wistfully across the ocean.

Her father, who was named Captain Flint Swift (Jnr) after his dad, was a handsome, strong man. Storm was certain that everyone would be a lot nicer to her mother and herself, if he were home more often.

Storm sat with Grandad Flint and her mother at the dining table overlooking the black rocks and foaming dark blue sea.

"You can't beat a jacket potato." Her mum's pretty face smiled as she passed cheese and salad around. She obviously wanted to know how school had been but didn't like to ask in case it caused stress at the dinner table and put everyone off their food.

"Quick, easy and yummy." Storm quoted her mother, piling cheese and butter on her potato, mashing it into the steaming flesh. They often had jacket potatoes when her mum was working on an art project as she became completely absorbed.

"Any homework?" Grandad Flint asked casually, peering over his glasses and shaking pepper onto his potato. His eyes twinkled. He was quite a young grandad at fifty three, full of energy, with a keen inquisitive mind.

"Just a bit of English, Pops. But I've done it."

"What's the plan for this evening?"

"Going exploring"

He nodded with approval.

"Any news on Dad?"

"No. He's busy. He'll call in when he can." Her mother took a sip of wine, her eyes travelling across the waves as if searching for him.

Storm cleared away the dishes and stacked the dishwasher, before returning to her round bedroom that soared almost as high as the clouds. The evening was her own. Her mother was in her studio painting. She was working on an exclusive calendar of her most popular paintings she planned to sell to raise money for an armed forces mental health charity. In addition, she was working on seascapes for an art exhibition in Edinburgh in the autumn. Grandad Flint was in his study reading and enjoying a glass or two of port. Time for adventure.

Storm dressed for her mission. She wore black cargo trousers and stuffed the pockets with her phone, candles and matches. Slipping on a hoodie and trainers, she tied her long blonde hair up into a bun on the top of her head. Armed with a torch, she headed out. Running down the spiral staircase, she made her way through the kitchen and down steps into the vast dark cellar. It seemed like a good starting point for her adventure. The island was full of unexplored caves, and earlier that day when gathering potatoes for dinner, she'd spotted an iron ring underneath a potato sack. It looked like a large rectangular trap door, about one meter long and half a meter wide. She was keen to find out what was beneath it.

Flicking on the light she entered the cellar and made her way to the slate steps that led down to the lower level. The Light House sat majestically up on the top of a steep hill. The original builders from centuries past had made good use of ground beneath by digging deep and creating the double cellars. Puffin Island was old and Storm wondered what its true history was. Her mother had told her bedtime stories about the island as a child, but she'd presumed they were pure fiction.

Dragging the potato sack off the iron handle, she pulled at the black metal ring. It was cold to the touch but the door stayed firmly in place. Crouching, she noticed four small keyholes: one at the top and bottom, and two at the right side. Perhaps it led to yet another cellar?

Her imagination conjured up a smugglers' route that led from the cellar down to the sandy cove to the west of the island, or a priest's hole (a secret hiding place). But it was bound to be something boring like Grandad Flint's secret stash of the expensive port he was so fond of!

Where would the key be? There were keys for the outhouses somewhere. If only she could remember where they were kept. The mystery keys could be in the same place. Looking around the cellar, she began to search. A vast wine rack covered one wall to the left containing a wide variety of wines. A pile of onions and potatoes in paper sacks were stacked on the floor near the trapdoor. No keys there.

Scrutinising the shelves full of homemade blackberry jam, pickles, chutneys and pasta sauces, she shook her head in frustration. The keys might even be in Grandad Flint's office, which was out of bounds. Storm checked inside the two large freezers full of pies, curries, ice cream, pizzas and homemade meals, but still no sign of any keys.

Rubbing the feeling back into her numb fingers, she stared at the painting on the wall of Puffin Island that Grandad Flint had painted as a young man. He didn't like it. Apparently the perspectives were out, which meant he hadn't painted the size of the building and birds correctly. However, no one in the family would agree to him burning it, and so it had been banished to the dark cellar. Putting her head to the wall, she carefully pulled the bottom of the painting out. There behind it were two sets of keys hanging on small nails. One set looked familiar and must be for the out-buildings, but the other set she had never seen before. Four small keys and two larger brass keys on a ring. Hooking it off the nail, she felt excitement building in her belly. The painting of Puffin Island was renamed in her mind as the Keeper of Keys.

Inserting the small keys, they clicked open in sequence. Lifting the lid, it opened out on hinges resting to the floor. But what lay within was a total anti-climax. There below was an empty space with a wooden bottom the depth of a deep drawer. An unused storage space. But why lock it, and what were the two extra keys for? It made no sense. Grandad Flint was super organised. Everything he did in life had a purpose. Even, it seemed, the painting of Puffin Island that he despised had become the Keeper of Keys. Storm spotted a tiny corner of wood missing to the right side of the bottom of the space. Inserting her forefinger she pulled up a thin wooden veneer.

Underneath was a stone slab with a round key hole...the home of the fifth key. Placing the thin plywood covering to the side, she inserted the key into the lock with a shaking hand. One thing was for sure, no one went to this much trouble unless they were keeping a secret. Storm took a deep breath and turned the key. A loud click. Success! Pulling up the slab, she saw it was set in a metal frame with hinges for ease of entry to the murky space below.

A fierce smell of sea salt rushed to her nostrils, followed by the icy blast of air. Switching on the beam, she saw iron rungs embedded into the wall to her right. Wishing she'd brought the head torch in her room that she'd used at Air Cadets, she hesitated, wondering whether to go back and get it. Curiosity argued that the torch she had was sufficient. Dangling her legs into the creepy shadows, she prayed it wasn't the home of some weird sea creature. But surely Grandad Flint would have warned her when she said at tea that she was going exploring. Instead she had seen approval in his eyes.

As a veteran group captain in the military, he was the reason she'd joined Air Cadets, as he thought it might help with her anxiety, build confidence and resilience. Her dad, Captain Flint Junior, had also encouraged her, believing that it was important for her to be physically and mentally strong and able to take care of herself in life. Her attendance at Air Cadets had been pretty grim during the last two years as her anxiety spiked, but no one mentioned it. There were quite a few issues not being mentioned in their household recently, it seemed.

Her foot found the first rung and she almost jumped at the touch. Hesitating for a moment, she took a breath before gingerly lowering very slowly down the rungs. Stopping intermittently, she shone the beam of light below. A black rock floor was two steps down. Climbing down, she stood on the flat rock surface, shining the light down a passage.

The walls were cold to the touch but with no water residue. Shining the beam along the passage she came to a strange fork. The tunnel went straight on but there was an alcove in the rock wall with three thick slate steps that led down to another large slab with a black ring handle. This slab, however, contained no lock. Was the sixth key merely a spare or yet another mystery to uncover?

Glancing at her phone, she saw it was already 8pm. She needed to be back in her room by 8:45 to dye her hair and be in bed by 10 o'clock. Grandad Flint and her mother were strict about lights out and plenty of sleep. It was part of her anxiety management. Apparently sleep helped. The tunnel or the slab? She decided that the tunnel might go on for miles and so that would be for another day, when she had time to explore properly.

Jumping down the steps, she hauled at the iron ring. The slab made a grating sound and moved upwards. Below were craggy steps downwards. Walking down she came to a door that appeared to be a man-made addition with a water tight seal. It was locked. Excitement mixed with terror coursed through Storm. What was beyond the door? Perhaps she should wait until Jenny or Holly were with her. But everyone was so busy with school work, clubs and family. She inserted the sixth key into the lock but it wouldn't turn. Puzzled, Storm tried the fifth key instead.

There was a loud click. Clever. No one would think that the same lock had been used twice. The door opened and Storm walked into a massive glistening chamber. The beam of torchlight illuminated a vast pool, easily the size of a swimming pool. Storm stood staring in astonishment! Walking to the edge and peering below, she saw clear sea water and a white sandy bottom devoid of seaweed, rocks or sea creatures. Shining the beam around, she saw rock ledges and a sea passageway in the shape of an arch that went under the rock wall to her right, possibly leading to another chamber. Part of the hill The Light House sat on must be hollow and full of caves. Rippling the water with her hand, it felt cold and appeared to be about two meters in depth. She had her own personal swimming pool!

The island was magical! Secret chambers, swimming pools, old passageways to explore, and still one other key with no lock accounted for. Time glared at her. It was 8:50pm. She had to go. Sighing with irritation, she retraced her steps, locking doors and replacing slabs as she went. One thing was certain...she would be back tomorrow as soon as she could, and this time she would be properly kitted out; her kit list now included her swimsuit, goggles, towel, flask of hot chocolate and a snack.

Standing once more in the cellar, she replaced the potato sack over the trap door and returned the keys behind the old painting of Puffin Island, the Keeper of Keys.

CHAPTER 5

Suspension

After giving her mother and Grandad Flint a hug goodnight, she ventured up the spiral staircase into her round bedroom. Her cat Marmite sat mournfully at the doorway glaring at Marmalade, who sat smugly on the red fluffy blanket on her bed, washing his face. The cats refused to sleep in the same room as they had when kittens and so were forced to take it in turns to snuggle up to Storm. Marmite in contrast to Marmalade, was a black cat with bright green eyes. She picked him up and gave him a cuddle. Putting him down she glanced at the hair dye and hesitated considering the enormity of what she was about to do. The last thing she wanted was to upset her mother, but it was the only solution she could think of to get out of going to school.

Storm left her room and went down the seven steps that led to her private bathroom that was also situated in the lighthouse tower. The bathroom was white marble with towel dryer, freestanding roll top bath and shower, toilet and sink. A row of five windows gave a breath-taking view of the bay. They hadn't always lived so affluently and Storm appreciated how fortunate she was. She laid old towels on the floor and suite just in case the dye splattered everywhere. Following the instructions she applied two boxes of hair dye to her long blonde hair.

The result when dry was a dark emerald green like wet seaweed. The colour completely altered her appearance, bringing out the green in her olive eyes. Pouting she took a selfie. The school were not going to be happy; but then that was the point. Putting her clothes out for the morning, she added a wool hat. Fortunately, the weather forecast was wind and rain, and she could feasibly hide her hair under the hat, without questions being asked.

Storm sat in registration, quivering inside, purposely ignoring the aghast expressions from her classmates, whispering and laughing. Her fellow students fidgeted, awaiting hell to rain down upon Storm. They were not disappointed. The teacher, Ms Young, strode in dressed in a long floral calf-length dress, green tights with flat leather sandals. She had an extraordinary dress code. Ms Young scanned the room to gauge attendance and almost stopped in her tracks upon spotting Storm.

She was shocked on two counts. The first that she was actually there, and secondly her dyed hair! Her usually sallow complexion went pink, clashing horribly with her light red hair. A battle seethed within Ms Young as she trembled with outrage. She bit her tongue, not wanting to give attention to deliberate bad behaviour. Her temper won the day.

"You," she exploded, pointing at Storm, "flouting school rules with your usual disregard! What did I say yesterday? What did I say?"

Several of the students murmured disapproval at the teacher's comments. Storm's sporadic attendance was due to mental health issues, not misbehaviour, but Ms Young in her temper had disclosed that deep down she obviously viewed them to be the same.

Ms Young went puce realising her error. The prospect of lawsuits and investigations danced around her brain. Thirty witnesses. Sixty pairs of glaring eyes.

"I meant dying your hair is deviant behaviour!" She spluttered. "Go to the Head's office now"!

Storm wove her way through the wooden desks to the door and out into the corridor. The road to freedom lay ahead with only a few hours left to endure!

"What is the meaning of this?" Ms Temple demanded, gesturing to Storm's dark green hair. "You had lovely blonde hair. Why would you dye it green of all colours?" Ms Temple was middle aged and glamourous. Her blonde curls sat on her shoulders framing her large blue eyes, high cheekbones and red lips. She wore a designer black and white dress with matching shoes. Expensive perfume hung in the air of the quiet room, situated next to her office. The room had been created for consultations with parents, or if something awful happened and peace and quiet was needed.

"I've phoned your mother and she's on her way! I appreciate that you're having problems," she added gently, "but the school has very strict rules when it comes to make-up, hair, and uniform. Surely you know that? Or is that why you did it?"

Storm nodded. The pain in her stomach was building with intensity. Sweat clung to her palms and suddenly the room darkened and her vision went fuzzy. It was like the beginning of an episode of *Dr Who;* she felt as though she was travelling down a whirling black hole. Ms Temple's voice echoed in her ears, and suddenly her fear erupted and she vomited over the light blue calming carpet and Ms Temple's shoes. Ms Temple immediately reached for a buzzer on the wall to summon back up.

As if by magic, Storm's mother appeared in the doorway with Nurse Pinch and the school receptionist. The caretaker was called to clean the carpet and the head's shoes, and gym trainers arrived for the head teacher to wear in the meantime. Rapid secret conversations were held by 'responsible adults,' and Storm's Mother led her wobbling from the room. Outside, Storm started crying. The last words she heard were:

"I'm sorry, Mrs Swift, but despite her anxiety issues, she has clearly broken school rules on purpose. We have no choice but to suspend her for two weeks at least. We can't be seen to give certain pupils preferential treatment or they'll all be coming in with purple, green and red hair." Ms Temple shuddered patting her own pretty blonde curls. "Obviously we'll have to have a meeting before she's allowed to return. Personally, I do understand, and the school will help Storm in any way we can."

"Of course. Sorry about her hair. Sorry about your shoes."

Storm could now take a breath. Two weeks was surely enough time to convince her mother to allow her to be homeschooled. She'd prove that she could do the school work at home, and better. Then she'd never have to go back. Her mother was worried about friendships and Storm's social interaction. She'd show her that she had nothing to be concerned about.

Climbing into the car, she looked at her mother's stressed face.

"Sorry Mum."

Her mother patted her knee absentmindedly and drove out of the carpark through the stone pillars, narrowly missing grating the paint off the right side of the car.

"Something needs to be done," she murmured.

Storm went to her bedroom upon returning home. Hugging Marmite to her chest, she felt soothed by his warmth and rhythmic purring. She felt exhausted. She had no more fight left in her. Her mother had gone straight into Grandad Flint's study. Twenty minutes later, a text message arrived from her mother: "Can you come down to the dining room please."

Her mother sat at the table drinking wine, even though it was 11:50 am, which wasn't even lunch time. Grandad Flint smiled and poured them both some tea out of a large blue and white tea-pot with matching cup and saucers.

Storm spoke first.

"I'm sorry. For the stress."

"This school issue must be horrible for you Storm; we appreciate that." Grandad Flint glanced at her mother. "You have mentioned in the past that you want to be homeschooled. We kind of thought, if you kept going to school, the anxiety may pass. It does for quite a few kids with this issue, you know. If you keep battling it and meeting it head on. It does lessen and eventually go away."

Storm shook her head furiously.

"It's not passing. I've tried. I promise. I can't do this anymore. It's exhausting!" Storm's voice trembled. "It's not the same for everyone! That's what no one gets!" Storm lowered her head onto her arms and sobbed. "I can't. I just can't."

"Storm, Grandad Flint and I have been having a conversation about all this." Her mother soothed, trying to calm the situation.

"We just wanted you to try. You have. The fact you were sick today, pretty much says it all," said Grandad Flint as he ran his fingers through his thick black hair streaked with grey. "I will speak to the school from now on as they seem to be giving your poor mother a rotten time. We'll trial home school and keep the school and social services in the loop. The head, Ms Temple's onside and has offered to help with anything needed."

Storm sat up. She couldn't believe what she was hearing. She wiped her eyes and nose on her navy blue school jumper.

Eyes full of concern looked back at her.

"You're going to have to stick to your end of the bargain though, Storm." Her mother took a sip of wine. "School's not for everyone. A lot of pupils don't like it, but have to just get on with it. Be assured that home school isn't going to be easy either. You still have to do the work and be self-motivated. Grandad Flint said he'll take charge of it as he has more time at the moment. We're lucky we're in a position to offer this or God knows what would happen. But you start mucking about..!"

"I won't. I promise."

"So the hair? " Grandad Flint asked.

"Desperation?" Her mother enquired.

Storm nodded.

"You better work hard and help out around the house!" Her mother added.

"I promise. And thanks for understanding." Storm hugged her mum and Grandad Flint and shot up the spiral staircase to her room. Lying down on the bed she felt relief flowing out of her. Some might see her behaviour as spoilt or manipulative, but they didn't understand the enormity of the problem that she had. It felt as if the weight of the world had been lifted off her young shoulders. Finally she was free.

CHAPTER 6
The End of the Tunnel

The next day was Saturday. Storm got up early and after a quick shower, prepared for further exploration. She packed her black rucksack with towels, swimwear, and other supplies and headed for the kitchen to make a flask of hot chocolate. Adding a cheese and pickle sandwich and crisps, she texted her mother that she was going exploring and would see her later before disappearing back into the lower cellar. The Keeper of Keys now took on a new meaning. Glinting keys hung innocently from the old nails, with the old painting of Puffin Island guarding their secrets. Storm replaced the trapdoor to the entrance of the tunnel. It was heavy but she was strong enough. This was her own private adventure and it felt good.

The head torch made it easier to climb down into the passageway and in no time she was standing once more at the fork. Which way should she go, right or left? The chamber with the pool beckoned. Storm was a strong swimmer and she'd completed her life saving and swimming certificates. She was eager to know where the arch in the swimming pool wall led to and to try out the newly discovered swimming pool. But where did the long passage go? She decided to head that way first.

The passage was straight and then dipped down a slope. Then veered to the right, then the left, then upwards. Then downwards again. It consisted of black rock that felt cold but was dry. After walking for five minutes, three recesses appeared, one on the right and two on the left. Shining the torch, she saw doorways boasting thick antique oak doors. Two were open.   Cautiously tiptoeing forward she glanced into the right hollowed room. Why she was tiptoeing she wasn't sure... It appeared to contain diving and camping equipment. Walking in, she saw it was a good size space with a wooden rack full of towels, bed linen and a bed. How weird! Storm wondered where the air came from as it was musty, but not unbearably so. It was certainly a strange place to situate an airing cupboard, or to house guests.

The second door to the left was also open. It was a larger room and the rocky walls were covered in old paintings and tapestries of biblical scenes. A silk lilac and silver Turkish rug covered the floor. An ornate golden bed engraved with Celtic symbols dominated the space, surrounded by rolls of exotic carpet, lanterns and old chests. Paintings were stacked against the side of a huge cupboard, packed full of candles, matches, tins of beans, soup, crackers, canned meats and crisps. Storm picked up a tin of baked beans. The sell-by date was '2022'. It was in date! A small camp stove sat at the bottom of the cupboard.

Storm dithered for a moment, wondering whether to bolt back to the safety of her bedroom. Sense told her that all of this must belong to Grandad Flint and maybe connected with her dad's work. The caves may have been used as a bomb shelter years ago during various wars, and later been converted for storage.

Lifting the lid of one of the trunks she saw it contained old books. Taking out a burgundy book with gold edged pages, she glanced at the spine of the book: *Treasure Island,* by Robert Louis Stevenson. Opening it, it had her dad's name on the first page: 'Flint Swift Jnr 1993'.

Storm expelled a long breath. Her heart pounded with excitement. The storage rooms were quite a discovery and totally unexpected. The contents were obviously family heirlooms. It had crossed her mind initially that pirates, people smugglers or even terrorists had found their way into the depths of Puffin Island and were using it for gain. It was a relief to know that evil wasn't lurking beneath her home.

However, the third door on the right was locked, and Storm didn't have a key to unlock it. The sixth key was too small to fit the keyhole. The Keeper of Keys may be hiding it. However she hadn't noticed any large heavy keys. Mystery was the dish of the day. The allusive key could be anywhere. Anyway, today's mission was to uncover the destination at the tunnels' end. The locked door would have to wait.

She continued her quest. The tunnel sloped up-hill. The torch threw out a yellow beam that bent upwards as the passage reached a dead end. Iron rungs were again embedded in the rock, providing a ladder to the top. Climbing, she saw a keyhole in the slab above her head. Inserting the sixth key, there was a twist and click. Storm breathed out slowly and gradually lifted it up. There was a small space and four key holes, a replica of the trapdoor in the cellar. The four locks clicked open with the small keys, but in a different sequence.

It was quite fiddly trying to remember which key she'd already used, especially in the dim light. The trapdoor was heavy and groaned as she moved it. Daylight illuminated the tunnel, and she gasped, blinking, as light and a strong smell of fresh air and salt invaded her nostrils. Her eyes adjusted quickly, and she clambered through the space into the interior of what she realised was the boathouse cabin.

The stone cabin attached to the actual boat-house was situated opposite Puffin Island. It belonged to the Swift's and housed the motorboats used for crossing over to the island. Storm stood in the large living room. A small rug was attached to the top of the trapdoor to disguise it.

The cabin was snug, containing a wood burner, leather sofas, thick red and orange rugs. Seascapes of stormy seas, hung from the walls. There was a small kitchen, bathroom and bedroom. Family and friends used it when they came to visit if they wanted to stay on the mainland. The discovery of what she now called the Tunnel of Freedom, the Emerald Pool Chamber, and the three rooms made her wonder what was the real purpose for those visitor stays at the boathouse cabin, but she was possibly overthinking.

Grandad Flint's twinkling blue eyes had displayed approval when she told him she was going exploring. If there were sinister activities going on, he would have warned her against it. Maybe the knowledge of the mysteries below Puffin Island were there only for the curious. "Adventure and discovery are to be pursued and achieved by individual desire and motivation. How else are people to grow and progress?" Her dad's voice echoed in her thoughts.

Now she had a direct route to the mainland and the beach. This gave her freedom of movement, for currently she was reliant on her mother to take her via the motorboat, dependent on the weather. Storm decided to return to the Emerald Pool Chamber where she would have lunch, and process the morning's discoveries. Carefully closing the trapdoor, she locked the entrance to the boathouse cabin and made her way back down the tunnel.

Sitting in the Emerald Pool Chamber, as she had officially named it, Storm lit candles placing them on the ledges surrounding the green pool. Pulling a blanket from her bag, she sat in comfort drinking steaming hot chocolate. The rich flavour and warmth hugged her. Biting into the cheese and pickle sandwich, she realised she was ravenous.

Storm's dark world now contained streaks of light. Overnight, anxiety, stress and dread connected to school had dissolved and a new way of living lay ahead. It had been an eventful week. First discovering the mysteries that lay beneath the island, then the school suspension, and finally her family stepping in, offering homeschooling, understanding and support.

Dying her hair the colour of wet seaweed had been a desperate cry for help and a massive gamble. But, if she hadn't done it, she'd be sitting in her lighthouse bedroom right now, worrying about the week ahead, immersed in dark negative fearful thoughts. Instead, on Monday, she had lessons at 8am with Grandad Flint at home on Puffin Island! It hadn't quite sunk in.

Her friend Jenny had often tried to reassure her.

"When you're sitting at the bottom of the pit, things can only get better. Sometimes you just need a leg up to the first rung. At the top there's a world full of light and hope you can't imagine at the moment."

"Easy for you to say," Storm's gloomy response had been. "You read too many psych books."

Jenny wanted to be a counsellor when she left school, and Storm was the perfect subject to practise on as she was so messed up.

"Never give up, Storm."

Jenny's wise words stayed with her, although she hadn't believed them, genuinely thinking that the dark pit was to be her home for eternity. But now there were flashes of brilliance and hope. It was a completely new experience, and her feet were literally climbing rungs   out of the tunnel, as well as the metaphoric pit. She smiled to herself.

Storm took out her phone. Two bars! How can that be! A signal down in the depths of the earth. Storm laughed, and the light happy sound bounced off the walls. The underground world and The Lighthouse Tower were her safe havens. New beginnings. Finally she had somewhere she could relax and be herself. The Tunnel of Freedom would help with her friendships as she could meet up with her friends whenever she wanted. Happy days!

The Emerald Pool beckoned. Changing into her swimsuit, she lowered herself tentatively into the water. It felt cold, but not unbearable. After a minute her body adjusted and she placed goggles over her eyes and swam up and down. The underwater arch in the chamber wall bothered her though. There could be anything lurking beyond it, some weird sea creature or worse.

Storm wasn't a fan of the dark, fish or bugs.

Clambering out of the pool, she made her way back to the room that contained the diving equipment.   There was a holdall with masks and torches. She saw her dad's military service number on the side. So, the equipment was his!

She borrowed three lanterns and an underwater flashlight and returned to the pool. The chamber, lit by candlelight, gave the impression of a luxurious spa that her mother would pay a lot of money to attend. It was cool, but Storm needed to explore further before she could relax and enjoy it. Re-submerging, she swam under the water. The underwater torch gave off a powerful beam that showed up the black crag of the pool walls and the glistening white sand of the sea bed. Through the archway she could make out a green tendril that looked like a seaweed finger beckoning her in. Storm wondered if there was an underwater camera with her dad's military equipment. How cool would that be!

Swimming to the underwater archway, the light illuminated a jungle of foliage in the distance. Breaking the surface of the water, she gasped for breath. She hovered, treading water. To swim through the archway was to leave the safe haven of the chamber. An exciting but scary prospect. Her phone buzzed and she swam back to her bath sheet and poured herself a hot drink. Steam rose. Wrapping herself in the thick towel, she realised that she was freezing cold.

A text message appeared. It was from her cousin Finn. He was fifteen, a year older than Storm. His mother was Storm's father's sister. Finn was clever and mature for his age. They currently lived in Gravestone, England, having moved there six months ago. Aunt Molly had separated from Josh, Finn's dad, and met a new man they called 'John the Psycho'. Finn hated it in Gravestone and loathed his step-dad.

"Storm, you about later?" the message said.

"Yes. You ok?"

"So so. Tell you later. Need to talk."

"Massive catch-up needed."

"Talk later. You on the island?"

"Yeah. You ok?"

No answer. He'd probably had a row with John, his stepdad, again. Storm was worried about him as he used to be loud, bubbly and confident. In the last year he'd become quiet, withdrawn and serious.

If Finn was with her they would be swimming and exploring the archway by now. She missed him a lot. He was clearly miserable. The last time they'd spoken he talked of rows with his stepdad and that he suspected John the Psycho was being abusive and violent to his mother. Seemed things hadn't improved. Maybe he'd be allowed to come and stay for a bit. Aunty Molly might enjoy a change of scene too.

Diving into icy water, Storm swam renewed determination. Questions would be asked later, and Storm didn't want to tell Finn she'd been too scared to explore. She decided to swim through the space as far as she could, using half her held breath. She needed to be careful in case the archway was a long tunnel and she needed to go back. The last thing she needed was to drown just as her life was taking a turn for the better.

CHAPTER 7

The Creepy Cave

Storm practised breathing exercises sitting on the sandy floor of the Emerald Pool and holding her breath for as long as possible so she could maximise her time spent underwater.

Switching on the head torch she duck-dived downwards, swimming through the arch and arriving into a dome-shaped air pocket. The finger of fern-coloured seaweed invited her to explore further and, taking a breath, she followed its thread, again swimming through icy dark shadows.

The distance of the tunnel was about two meters, and leaving the stone confinement she swam out into the water. Storm judged that the depth was around four meters as she was now swimming upwards and running out of breath fast.

Her body braced as a tall dark shape loomed through the murky fog. Startled, Storm flapped her arms. She had no breath left in her body. In sheer panic, she propelled her body to the surface, cursing her stupidity. Passing port-holes crusted with grey coral, limpets, sea anemone and a million other small sea creatures, terror gripped her as the image of a ghost ship emerged nearer with each stroke. Out of breath and swallowing sea water she strained upwards.

Finally, breaking the surface, she gasped for breath, choking and coughing, her eyes streaming. Treading water, she swam, gripping the rocky wall, heaving sea water whilst greedily filling her lungs with air once more.

Ripping her torch from the pouch on her belt, she flashed the yellow circular beam around the chamber. The relief of light illuminated a sorry sight. An old battered wreck sat stranded and moored for eternity. It was half sunk but wedged firmly on the rocks beneath.

Storm's pulse lessened and her breathing returned to normal. She couldn't believe how stupid she'd been. Fancy, presuming that the Creepy Cave was the same depth of water. It was a harsh lesson learnt.

"Idiot!" Her voice echoed throughout the chamber.

Things were getting more sinister by the minute. Anxiety hammered at her. She could have died. What if the water had been deeper, she'd have drowned for sure. It didn't bear thinking about.

Storm practised yoga breathing to calm down as her panic was threatening to spiral out of control. Logically this was a scary situation, so her anxiety was justified. This wasn't the same as the emotion she felt at school.

In a macabre way this pleased her. She was experiencing a normal healthy terror, not a fight or flight subconscious reaction. She had definitely turned a corner in her recovery.

Judging by the formation of the rocks and the distant noise of the sea, Storm supposed that the old ship had been driven into the cave by a wild sea many moons ago and later been entombed there by a massive rockfall that had completely covered the entrance to the chamber. Pulling herself up onto a sandy ledge, she sat viewing her surroundings.

Storm shivered involuntarily.

"That was scary," she whispered to herself. "Scary. Scary," her voice echoed back at her like a phone conversation with a bad signal. A ledge ran around the chamber, broken only by a heap of boulders, clustered where the entrance to the cave had once been. Storm wished Finn or one of her friends was with her. The sight of the old wreck was daunting and made her feel slightly sick.

The masts were long gone, probably broken off on entry, rotted, and been eaten by creatures. Storm decided to call the chamber the Creepy Cave. The Emerald Pool Chamber was a very different place. It was serene, tall and majestic, with its clear green water and sandy bottom.

Storm had no idea what lurked in the misty waters of the Creepy Cave and was very reluctant to return to the icy blackness. She'd had a few scuba diving classes during the school holidays. Maybe there was scuba diving apparatus with her dad's kit. If so, it would be needed. She decided to invite Finn to come and stay for a while when she spoke to him later. He would love this.

Storm forced herself to be brave and stood up on shaky legs. Needing to warm up, she walked the loop around the chamber, scrutinising the wreck, checking out the glistening walls and terrifying sea pool. No doors or passageways revealed themselves, and the depth showed the ship and rocks below. It was as she thought, simply an adjoining cave and rockfall.

The location of the Creepy Cave was probably westward, if she stood on the mainland beach looking at Puffin Island. Later she'd explore the area above ground. Storm's teeth chattered with cold, and refastening the large torch to her belt, she decided the fastest way to return at speed to the Emerald Pool Chamber and conserve breath, was to dive in.

Cutting through the water, she swam rapidly down until she spotted the archway below. Taking a breath in the middle point that she now called the Dome of Breath, she returned to the Emerald Pool. The chamber looked familiar and safe after the Creepy Cave. Relief and exhaustion flooded her. Wrapping herself in the towel, she drained the remainder of the hot chocolate and munched a packet of cheese and onion crisps, before getting changed back into dry clothes.

Arriving back in the cellar, Storm hid the keys behind the painting of Puffin Island. It was 5pm and her turn to make dinner. Opening the freezer, she decided on a homemade chicken and ham pie with chips and salad as she was too tired to cook anything elaborate. Placing the pie and fries in the oven, she set the table for three people in the dining room. The smell of pie drew Grandad Flint and Storm's mother out of the study and studio.

"Smells great," said Grandad Flint, rubbing his hands. Sitting down, he passed around the rocket, tomatoes and cucumber.

"How's your painting going, Mum?" Storm asked, taking a mouthful of pie.

"Good," Lily nodded, "tomato sauce anyone? I got a bit stuck earlier on. This wretched wave. It just didn't look right. But I'm happy with it now. Took ages! About four hours!"

"I don't have the patience for painting anymore," said Grandad Flint taking a sip of red wine. "Not that I was ever that good. How was your exploration, Storm?"

"Good. Yeah. Found some cool caves and rocks, interesting."

Storm skirted around the subject of where she'd been exploring. She had found cool caves and rocks so she hadn't lied. She just hadn't said where.

What a day!

After dinner, Storm sat in her bedroom looking out of the large window at the gun metal grey waves with white tips speeding inland. Bad weather was imminent. The wind howled around the lighthouse and the lamp was already flashing a warning to ships to ward them away from the hidden black rocks that would rip their hulls to shreds as they had the Ghost Ship. Calling Finn, she got no answer and left him a voice-mail and text.

Climbing the stairs to the Zen viewing room and lounge area situated about four meters below the lamp, she looked out across the island. The walls were made of toughened reinforced glass and were in fact vast windows from floor to ceiling. The area was furnished with a soft cream sofa, colourful lamps and lanterns, thick rugs, bean bags and a log burner.

Storm loved it there, and often lay staring out across the ocean listening to music or reading. There were black-out blinds in all the rooms for when the lamp was on. The Zen room was a favourite of Marmite, as he liked the warmth, especially in the summer when the sun beamed in. The windows wouldn't open as it was too high and dangerous, but there were air vents.

Still no response from Finn. Grabbing a thick black hoodie she pulled on her army boots and ventured out. The wind hit her, and for a moment she staggered backwards. Pulling the door shut she headed to the west side of the island. Securing her hair inside the hoodie she pulled the drawstring tight. It wasn't the ideal weather for exploring as the wind was about twenty five miles per hour with a cold chill, but Storm felt restless after the day's events.

The tide was in, covering part of the sandy beach. Most of the caves along this section of the island were just dead-ends. Cliffs eroded by the sea. Next time in the Creepy Cave, she'd pay more attention to the roof area. Maybe there was an old natural passageway before the rocks caved in.

A message appeared on group chat from her friend Holly telling them that she'd won the regional gymnastic competition and been put forward for the nationals. Holly was totally committed and practised for hours every day. Storm typed congratulations and how proud of her she was. Jenny responded too, adding that she was free in a couple of weeks for a catch up. Storm checked her cousin Finn's location on snapchat, but nothing. His snapchat emoji that looked so like him, with his shock of black hair, brown skin tone, and dark blue eyes was absent from the snapchat map. Maybe his locations were turned off.

Walking to the end of the beach she examined the terrain. There was one cave that had random rocks piled at what could have been an entrance. However the Creepy Cave was below water level. She was pretty certain of that, so she wasn't even sure what she was looking for. Storm admitted that swimming through the archway into the unknown water full of sea-weed, creatures and the ghost ship had spooked her and she was loathe to repeat it. Really she was hoping to find an easier access point. Climbing up a mini cliff, she stood on grass now facing northwest. Rock pools littered this aspect of the island. The east end was a popular nesting area for gannets, puffins and other gulls. They kept away from certain areas of the island as much as possible during the nesting season. The shrill cry of seagulls echoed above her.

"I wonder!" She said out loud. Her eyes scanned the numerous pools.

One of the rock pools was about five foot deep with a slate floor. She'd swum in it growing up when they visited Grandad Flint, before moving to Puffin Island. They used to live in army accommodation on a number of bases, before moving to a cottage in Shelley on the mainland, not far from the island.

Grandad Flint had asked them to move over to the island earlier in the year, and her mother had agreed straight away, as she was fond of Grandad Flint and was lonely at times, plus it was a fantastic place for her to paint. Storm suspected, her mother had hoped that the island would help cure Storm's anxiety. Storm had been thrilled to move to Puffin Island. What fourteen year old was going to say no to living on an island in a lighthouse tower with her own bedroom and private bathroom!

The island boasted a sandy beach, rock pools, a small forest, meadows and masses of volcanic rock. The south of the island narrowed into a strip, the middle section dipping down into the sea, reappearing when the tide went out. Storm made her way over to the strip of grass the size of a football pitch. She had weeded this area last week to rid it of tree mallow. Latin name: Lavatera Arborea, enemy of the Puffin, for it blocked their nesting holes. It grew up to three meters high with purple flowers and big woolly leaves. It must look like a terrifying giant to the tiny puffins. Interestingly, Marmite and Marmalade left the wild birds alone, playing only with the odd unfortunate mouse or vole.

Her phone rang. It was her mother. She sounded a bit strange as if she had a cold. Storm's stomach plummeted to ice. Had she been crying? Not her dad! She lived in fear of a phone call informing them he'd been killed in action or maimed.

"Have you heard from Finn, Storm?"

Equally bad. Not Dad but Finn. Storm tensed.

"What do you mean? Why?" She asked sharply. The wind buffeted the phone. "I can barely hear you. I'm coming in."

Her mother was sitting at the dining table staring out through the large picture window, drinking red wine. The wood burner was lit. Purple and orange flames flickered bringing colour, warmth and cheer into the light room.

"Is he missing?" Storm burst into the room. "I called him earlier. He's not got back to me."

"Did he say anything?" Her Mother's eyes were serious. It was not the time for pretence.

"Just that he needed to talk. He's worried, I think about his mum Aunt Molly."

"Go on," Grandad Flint limped into the room and sat down at the table.

Storm fiddled with her phone. Finn had told her his concerns in confidence. However, if his step-dad John had done something awful to Finn or his mum, she needed to tell them what she knew.

"He doesn't get on with his step-dad John. He's worried he's being violent to Aunty Molly. He said he's always shouting and swearing at her."

Her Mother's eyebrows shot up and she exchanged glances with Grandad Flint. They obviously weren't surprised by this information.

"He is ok, isn't he? Finn?" Storm looked wildly from her mother to Grandad Flint, daring one of them to lie to her. "I'm not a child; please just tell me what's going on!"

"No one thinks you're a child, Storm," Grandad Flint said calmly.

"Aunt Molly called. Finn's disappeared. Apparently John and Finn had a fight yesterday and it was a bad one. He must have left in the night. She's obviously really worried and your dad's on his way back to help find him. We're pretty sure Finn's on his way here."

"Obviously Finn's only fifteen, underage and it's dangerous for him to be out alone," added Grandad Flint.

"He must have had good reason," Storm said defensively. "He adores his mum, and he's scared for her. Things must have been grim for him to leave."

"If you hear anything, Storm?"

"Of course. Will he be sent back to Gravestone?"

"I've asked Aunty Molly to come stay for a few weeks. Sounds like she needs a break from there anyway. If Finn's run from an abusive situation he certainly won't be sent back," said Grandad Flint

Storm nodded and returned to the Zen room. Looking out across Shelley, she willed Finn to get in touch. Where was he?

CHAPTER 8
Bad weather and a rescue

The wind growled around the lighthouse tower at speed. Howling, it raced and roared around Puffin Island driving rain onto the windows like a thousand fingernails tapping to come in. Storm had fallen asleep to nature's orchestra about 10pm, exhausted by the day's events.

She arose from her bed and walked in the pitch blackness down the spiral staircase that led directly into the Emerald Pool Chamber. A candle appeared, hovering in mid-air, illuminating the cavern. Marmalade sat in the chamber on a ledge watching her as she dived into the water. It felt warm like a heated swimming pool, and she swam down to the sandy bottom that began to spin like a whirlpool, faster and faster, sucking her in. Whizzing along a golden tunnel, it spat her out and she landed inside the sinister innards of the ghost ship.

She appeared to be in a watery cabin. A gold chair and table were surrounded by ancient chests. The lid of one of the chests opened before her eyes, and out swam a laughing emerald mermaid with glinting eyes. She sat on the table and began flicking Storm with her tail showering her in water.

Storm awoke with a start. Her heart was pounding. Marmalade asleep next to her, sat up, and washed his orange tail, before settling back down to sleep. The window next to her bed was open, and droplets of rain had pelted onto her sleeping face. After the day's events she wasn't surprised her dreams were messed up.

Her phone was buzzing. It was Finn calling her at midnight.

A picture message appeared from him on messenger. His face was sporting a black eye and fat lip.

"Am okay. But that's me away now. Not going back. I've texted Mum I'm safe. Hopefully she'll go too, tried talking but she's not hearing me."

"Where are you? Everyone's worried sick." Storm quickly text back.

"Near but not going back."

Finn's location was still turned off. Storm sighed with frustration.

"You're not out in this?"

"Nah."

"Can I call you?"

No reply. Storm called his number but no answer.

Storm frowned. Finn was obviously worried he would be sent back to Gravestone. He didn't know about the secret tunnel, and he wouldn't want anyone journeying over to the mainland by boat in weather that was wild and dangerous.

From the Zen room, Storm gazed out in the direction of the boathouse. She had a strong feeling he was there. Although Finn still had school friends in Shelley, at this time of night there were limited places to go. It made sense that he would gravitate to Puffin Island.

Storm decided to go to the boat house via the tunnel where the elements couldn't touch her. However, this held less appeal at night than during the day, even though the tunnels were dark during daylight hours. The underworld of the island was a sinister and spooky prospect at the hour of midnight.

This was no time to be fearful. Her cousin was in trouble and needed her. Storm wished at that moment that Marmite and Marmalade were big fierce dogs instead of cute fluffy cats. The thought of travelling along cold dark tunnels alone was not appealing. Storm wondered whether to tell her mother that she'd heard from Finn; but, she probably already knew as Finn had texted his mum, and news travels fast. Besides, he might not even be at the boathouse.

Pulling on a thick navy hooded jumper over her grey pyjamas, she picked up her boots and tiptoed down the staircase, making her way along to the kitchen. Glancing out of the window she could see the dark sea foaming and churning as it hit the rocks, sending white spray high up into the air. It was a wild night. Storm slipped on her boots and went to the lower cellar, easing herself down into the tunnel. This time she left the entrance open. If she found herself in danger, it would be clear where she'd gone.

Trekking along the volcanic passageway that lay beneath the powerful ferocious ocean, Storm's every sense was on high alert.

'It's daylight out there. It's not midnight or super terrifying. Everything is fine!" she muttered to herself.

Her teeth chattered with fear and cold. Swinging the torch beam into the open storage rooms, she saw nothing had been disturbed. Taking a deep breath, she blew her breath out slowly calming her shredded nerves. Logic told her that the Emerald Pool Chamber and the Creepy Cave were inaccessible from the outside and this tunnel was the same. With the weather being the way it was, she was probably safer here than anywhere.

The light caught the edge of the thick locked door. A split second glance, but Storm could have sworn she saw the door closing - a micro fraction of movement! It must be the shadows, or her imagination playing tricks on her. Her first instinct was to run; but if she found Finn and brought him back down the tunnel she had to know that it was safe. Pulling at the black iron handle, she found the door was firmly locked as before. Storm swung the torchlight all around her. There was no one about. Her intuition argued that someone was lurking nearby. She was really losing it!

Reaching the end of the tunnel and climbing up the rungs, she cautiously opened the trapdoor. The boat house cabin was dark, empty and locked. Opening the back door that led from the kitchen into the actual boathouse, she encountered a pile of old potato sacks in the corner, but no Finn. Damn, she'd been convinced that he was there for some reason.

"Finn! It's Storm!" She shouted into the roaring icy wind, praying the gusts would carry her words to his ears.

A huge wave crashed against the doors of the boathouse making her jump. Both motorboats were absent. There should've been one tightly moored there. One was at the small boathouse on Puffin Island, but the other was missing. The doors of the boathouse banged loudly and a petrifying realisation hit her. Finn must have taken it to travel across the wild stormy sea to Puffin Island. Rushing outside the wind knocked her backwards. Rain hammered down onto her head and face. A thousand vicious painful pin pricks. She could just make out the white of the motorboat in the distance.

"No Finn no!" Storm shrieked.

The sea was heaving. He could easily capsize and drown.

It was a suicide mission.

She bolted back into the boathouse. The key to the motorboat was missing from behind the loose wood panel where it was kept. Racing into the cabin, she locked the door with shaking hands. Securing the trapdoor, Storm sprinted as fast as her legs would carry her through the tunnel, speeding up as she passed the thick locked door. Trying to catch her breath, she reached the rungs. Replacing the trapdoor, she hurled the keys behind the painting of Puffin Island and raced out to the quay.

The lighthouse lamp illuminated the waves intermittently, showing the small boat climbing and falling over the vast waves. Finn was no longer heading directly to the island but appeared to be drifting to the east. The roar of the wind was too loud for her to hear if the motor was running. It was clear that a strong current was carrying him out into the North Sea. Glimpses of orange and white emerged, Finn was wearing the life jacket that lived in the motorboat.

Rushing back into the house she yelled up the stairs. "Mum! Grandad Flint! Wake up!"

Storm banged the panic alarm. Sirens blasted through the house and the lamp light changed from white to red, alerting the coast guard and the sleeping occupants of the Light House. Switching on the powerful torch, she raced back to the quayside, screaming into the gale.

"I'll get a rope!" Storm ran to where the emergency lifebelt and rope were and tried throwing it out to sea, but Finn was too far out, and the wind savagely hurled it back to her.

Storm could just make out his face strained in concentration as he battled with the oars against the elements. Every time he got nearer to the island, giant waves propelled him away. Racing to the nearest point, Storm waded out over the submerged rocks. He was so near but it was clear he would miss the island completely. Torrential rain cascaded, making him a mere blur amidst the waves.

Storm couldn't get to him. The other motorboat was smaller and quite useless in bad weather. In this brazen sea it would be smashed to pieces on the rocks in seconds. Finn was drifting further away, the sea throwing him about like a cork on the tide. Storm had never known such terror, but was totally powerless. If help didn't arrive soon, Finn would drown at sea. Her mother was screaming at her to get out of the sea, and Grandad Flint was on the phone, both soaked to the skin in their night clothes and dressing gowns. Storm edged around to the east side of the island, waving and shouting comfort and encouragement at Finn.

Shaking with cold and adrenalin, she ran back to where the small motorboat was moored. Her mother raced after her.

"Storm, no!"

"He'll die!"

A droning and the sound of a helicopter's double rotators sounded in the distance, getting louder by the second.

Dots of yellow far away announced a boat ripping through the black water, but by the time they reached the island it would be too late for Finn. Running back to where she had last seen Finn, Storm screamed with anguish. The motorboat had capsized and was upside down. Finn bobbed by the side of it supported merely by his life jacket.

The drone increased to a deafening roar drowning out mother nature. Light and power filled the night sky as a Chinook helicopter cut its way at speed through the dark storm, beams flashing, searching the inky depth below.

"Dad! Oh my God, it's Dad! Finn, it's Dad!" Storm waved the torch frantically at Finn's location shouting and pointing. The powerful beam of the helicopter had already picked out her tiny form and was scanning the black heaving waves. Her mother and Grandad Flint stood next to her, dressing gowns flapping in the wind, praying for a miracle. They held their breath, for Finn was now lying face down in liquid ice.

Mere seconds had passed, but it seemed like hours.

The Chinook hovered for a moment, then moved out to sea. A rope appeared and a tall black figure zoomed down it swaying manically in the wind. The Chinook stopped on the hover and the figure bent, plucking an orange and black figure out of the sea.

Storm gasped and staggered backwards in fright as she saw Finn's lifeless figure, attached to her father hanging in mid-air. The capsized motorboat had disappeared, travelling on the waves to Denmark.

White dashes of rain fell relentlessly, but the wind had eased. The Chinook moved back to the island depositing them both on land near the house before moving back to the strip of land to the south-east of the island, and landing.

Storm, her mother, and Grandad Flint bent over against the airflow of the slowing rotator blades, racing to Finn and Flint Jnr.

A figure from the helicopter ran over.

"Tom's a medic!" Captain Flint Jnr shouted to his family. He was attempting CPR on Finn, as the medic covered him in a strange tin foil blanket and took over.

Pushing his chest, he blew air into his water filled lungs.

"Come on lad," he urged. "We're not giving up and don't you either."

It seemed to go on for-ever. They just stood watching his lifeless face, willing him to live. How could he still be alive? It seemed like days of waiting. Finn suddenly choked and threw up over and over, emptying his lungs of seawater. Sitting upright, he clutched hold of the medic's arm. Storm rushed to him and hugged him tightly.

The medic did several checks on Finn and then nodded.

"You're a fit young man. You'll live." He smiled and sat back on his heels with relief.

"Thanks, mate. You saved his life. I owe you one, and James," Flint Jnr said to the medic. They shook hands, and the medic returned to the helicopter. "James, thank you!" he called to the pilot, who gave him the thumbs up.

"It's okay now, Finn," Flint Jnr's deep voice rumbled through the night.

He turned and waved to the Chinook as the rotators droned and whizzed once more. It rose like a giant bee and disappeared into the night.

Grandad Flint returned to the Light House. Storm's mother helped Finn back into the house, followed by Storm and her father, who picked her up and hugged her like a child.

Grandad Flint was making tea and put cake and biscuits out.

Finn stood in the dining room staring at the flames dancing in the wood burner. He looked dazed and lost. Water dripped from his body onto the wooden floor. Storm cuddled him. He smelt of seaweed and was soggy. He clung to her.

"Storm, take Finn for a shower, and here's some clean clothes." Her mother handed her a pair of her father's black track trousers, socks and a cream hoodie and t-shirt. "You look soaked to the skin too."

"We'll meet back here in twenty minutes."

Finn nodded. He was clearly exhausted and looked drained. Reaching the bathroom, Storm touched his bruised face and gave him another cuddle. His arms closed around her tightly.

"Are you alright?" Storm pulled back looking at his swollen eyes.

"Apart from upsetting everyone, wrecking the boat and nearly drowning, you mean?" He shook his head.

"God I was so scared. If you die, I swear I will." Storm couldn't stop shaking.

"It was idiotic. I was so desperate!" Tears threatened, and Finn's bottom lip trembled with suppressed emotion. "I'm a bloody selfish idiot!" Storm handed him some toilet roll and he blew his nose loudly.

"You're okay now." Storm said, gently squeezing his arm.

"What about Mum? I just left her. With him. Who does that! And your dad? Where did he come from?"

"Aunty Molly phoned him when you went missing. He was heading back from Shetland to help look for you. Good timing. You must have a guardian angel looking after you, Finn. None of this is your fault. It's psycho John's. Maybe now your mum will come home too?"

"He won't let her." Finn shook his head.

"Won't be up to him if Dad gets involved. Get showered. We can talk later."

Finn looked terrible. He was tired and ashen faced.

"Are you hungry?"

"Starving, now you mention it…and bloody freezing."

"Hot shower will warm you. I'll get changed and make you some food. Tomorrow I'll take you on the grand tour of stuff I've discovered." Storm smiled. "If you're feeling up to it."

"If they let me stay. I actually feel okay. Which is weird as I nearly just died."

"Can't see Mum, Grandad Flint or Dad sending you back with a bruised face like that. They're your family too."

"I just didn't know what else to do. Couldn't stay there."

"Tell me about it."

Storm lowered the hood of her heavy wet blue jumper shaking out her long dark emerald hair.

"Oh wow. Now that is cool." He smiled. "I seriously dig that look on you."

"I didn't know what to do either."

CHAPTER 9
After the Storm

The family sat around the dining table. The storm had eased and quietened a little. The orange blue flames flickered in the wood burner and an array of scented candles on the mantlepiece brought cheer and warmth to the room.

Finn sat in front of the fire looking embarrassed. He looked Grandad Flint in the eye first before the rest of the adults.

"I'm sorry I caused so much bother and wrecked the boat. I'll pay for it somehow. Has anyone heard from Mum? I just left her with that psycho. Who does that?"

Flint Jnr spoke first. He sat back appraising Finn and Storm.

"Your mum made a mistake with John. It happens, but you got pulled into a toxic situation. You're mother's a grown up, and without meaning to talk down to you, you're fifteen, and had no say in the matter. Your actions may have been rash but we all understand why you did it".

"How!" Finn shouted. "I left her with a lunatic."

"You felt alone, scared and desperate. This has brought matters to a head. Now they have to be dealt with. Otherwise that situation could have gone on for years and got worse."

"Look at your face, Finn." Aunt Lily said. "That was just the start of it. It would have got worse and we don't yet know the full facts of what your mum's suffered at this man's hand."

The Alexa timer sounded. Storm sprang up from the table and

went to the kitchen, telling Alexa to be quiet.

Storm squirted some tomato sauce on chicken burgers with melted cheese and put them in seeded buns. Adding chips, she put cups of hot chocolate on the tray and took them to the dining room, placing the food in front of Finn and her dad, who were both famished. Her dad tugged her hood down and pulled out her hair that was tucked away. It hung in shiny dark green tresses down her back.

"So much has changed in the last six weeks since I went off on exercise," he grinned. "My daughter has become a mermaid, been suspended from school, and my nephew looks like he's done a round with Mike Tyson in the boxing ring, run away, and nearly drowned. My dad's broken his ankle clambering about the rocks clearing tree mallow. Lily?"

"Well I've nearly finished my collection, Flint," Lily smiled at him. "Been well behaved."

"Seems you're the only one." He took a bite of his burger.

"How did you get back?" Lily asked Finn.

"Nicked some money out of John's wallet while he was in the shower. Yeah, add theft to my crimes! Probably Mum paid the price for that too," he added gloomily. "I got a London to Edinburgh ticket but jumped the train up to London, and from Edinburgh to Shelley."

"At least you had the sense not to hitchhike." Lily added.

"Got soaked walking from Shelley to here. Storm kept calling but I didn't want her coming over to the mainland in that wee motorboat. It was too dangerous, and I knew she would've."

"But not too dangerous for you." Grandad Flint poured the adults a large brandy.

"I'm older and been working out at the gym and swimming a lot. I'm pretty fit now and thought I could handle the boat. Was sitting in the boathouse wet and freezing. I'd walked miles and was starving. Could see Puffin Island and I just thought....well I was an idiot. There's no excuse."

Finn wolfed down the food and drink. He clearly hadn't eaten for ages.

"You weren't far off. If the motor hadn't failed, maybe you would have made it. I've texted your mum. I'll get her tomorrow and bring her back. She's not mad, just relieved you're ok," Flint Jnr said.

"What about him? Psycho John." Finn looked worried. The left side of his face was swollen and his dark blue eyes were massive in his face. A purple bruise surrounded his eye.

"She's told him she has family business and has to head north for a few days. He agreed."

Finn raised his eyebrows. He clearly didn't believe it.

"And he's good with that. Really?"

"Your mum told him that her brother, meaning me, was coming to collect her from London but was happy to drive down to Gravestone, as he's on leave. That may have had something to do with him being okay with it."

"Go Dad. Even the thought of you is scary!" Storm burst out laughing.

"Oh I would love him to pick a fight with me. Believe me." He laughed.

"Typical bully. Picks on a small woman and a fifteen year old, but not a six-foot-two SAS solider," Storm said crossly.

"Yep. That's for sure," Finn nodded.

"Right, you two. Bed. Finn can sleep in the Zen room for now. I'll bring up some blankets," Aunt Lily said.

"Lessons now at 9am," added Grandad Flint with merriment. "Oh yes, Storm, I haven't forgotten tomorrow is a school day."

The birds were tweeting. It was 3:30 in the morning.

Storm and Finn went up to the Zen room. Her mother brought blankets and sat talking calmly to Finn, reassuring him that he wasn't going to be banished back to Gravestone. A pile of thick fluffy blankets sat on the sofa. Marmite immediately jumped onto the middle of them and began kneading furiously.

Tomorrow, after lessons, Storm planned to show Finn the new world beneath the Light House, the Emerald Pool Chamber and the Creepy Cave. Who knew what tomorrow would bring. Never a dull day on Puffin Island!

CHAPTER 10
An Overheard Conversation

Despite the eventful night, Storm woke up early. Finn was sleeping soundly in the Zen room, snuggled on the soft sofa bed with a contented smile on his face. Marmite was curled up beside him on the red thick fluffy blanket. Storm's tummy grumbled with hunger, and she took a quick shower and dressed in black and white yoga pants, top and hoodie. Adding trainers, she put her dark green hair up into a bun on the top of her head. Passing the steps that led up to Grandad Flint's study, she could hear her dad's deep voice rumbling alongside Grandad Flint's.

"It's frustrating I know, but at least he's safe." Her dad, Flint Jnr's voice.

"He's worried." Grandad Flint replied.

"I trust the kids. They're both great; but they're young people. If someone gets hold of them!"

"Probably best Finn's here." Flint Jnr said. "Ironically, when Molly called, I was on my way back anyway to collect them both. Word out that they are frustrated not knowing where Josh is, whether he's dead or alive, and may use other means to find out."

"Jeez, price on all their heads," Grandad Flint sounded outraged.

"He's too good a soldier. Did their organisation some damage. Coffee?" Her dad's voice travelled nearer.

Storm sped to the kitchen, flicking on the oven and the kettle. What on earth was all that about? Putting two waffles in the oven to cook, she broke an egg into the frying pan, digesting what she'd heard.

Had they been talking about Josh, Finn's dad? Josh was a strong man of African origin, hence Finn's dark olive skin. Over six foot tall, he was a skilled and determined man. He worked alongside her dad in Special Forces but had been missing in action for the last six months, or so they'd been told. Was he in hiding instead?

Molly and Josh's marriage had failed, and they'd been separated for over a year. Molly met John the Psycho when Josh was away working overseas, and not long after, moved down south, dragging a reluctant Finn with her. That's when all the trouble had started. Storm decided to keep the information to herself for now. There was no point dishing out false hope.

CHAPTER 11
Shipwrecks and Exploration

After breakfast, Storm sat at the dining room table with Grandad Flint.

"I thought we'd start off with History as that's the first subject on your actual school time table for today."

"About that, Pops. Can it be any history?"

Grandad Flint scratched his head.

"Suppose so, today, as it's the first lesson. Something in mind?"

Her father came in and ruffled her hair. "Popping down to London to pick up Molly." He kissed her on the cheek and sat down next to his dad, stretching out his long legs. They looked so alike with their dark tousled hair, dark blue eyes and regular features, only Grandad Flint had deeper laughter lines and streaks of silver in his hair. "You alright?" He asked Storm smiling at her.

"I am now." She said referring to the school situation.

"Good. Back tonight. We'll have some catch up time soon, Storm," he nodded getting up.

"Stay safe," Storm said.

"Always."

After her dad left, they sat discussing the lesson.

"I'm interested in knowing a bit about here." She gestured out of the window to the Firth of Forth. "Shipwrecks, that sort of thing."

Grandad Flint gave her a strange look; his eyes pierced into hers for a second, as if he was attempting to access her thoughts. Then he smiled. "Well, I know that there's about five hundred wrecks down in the Firth of Forth," Grandad flint began, "but one in particular may interest you." He took a sip of coffee. "Now this is a true story. Oh, morning Finn! Care to join us?"

Finn walked into the dining room with a cup of coffee and a bowl of Cocoa Pops. He was dressed in grey track trousers and a hoodie. His dark hair stood on end.

"Sure. What's the lesson?"

"Shipwrecks!" Storm volunteered.

"Oh cool." He took a loaded mouthful of cereal.

"You okay after your ordeal?" Grandad Flint asked.

Finn chewed quickly and swallowed.

"Yeah, thanks, Pops. I slept really well. Just starving."

"Well help yourself to whatever you want. Larder and freezers are well stocked and this is your home too."

"Cheers, Pops; that's good to know."

"Uncle Flint has gone to get your mum, so everything's alright."

Finn nodded. He looked relieved.

"On with the lesson. I think you'll enjoy this too, Finn. In 1633, a treasure-laden ship called the Blessing of Burntisland, a royal ferry belonging to Charles I sank during a storm whilst carrying Charles I's possessions across the Firth of Forth. This was shortly after he'd been crowned King of Scotland. Apparently, only 2 of 35 people on board survived. The king watched from his own ship, the Dreadnought. That was 366 years ago. Since then, hundreds of divers, the Royal Navy and all sorts, have been searching, trying to find the lost treasure, but without success. It is believed to contain a 280 piece silver dining service commissioned by King Henry VIII, as well as other royal possessions, which today would be worth 500 million pounds."

"Oh wow!" Finn and Storm exchanged glances.

"This for real?" Finn asked.

"This is for real. Furthermore, the historical significance of the ship was enormous. Charles I was pretty upset after his treasure sank into the sea. So much so that he rounded up nineteen witches in Lancashire, blaming them for creating the storm and a surge of waves that sunk the vessel. However, it most likely sank because it was overloaded with treasure and weighed too much. The treasure at that time was said to be worth 100,000 pounds, which back then was one fifth of the entire Scottish exchequer.

"Blimey!" said Finn. "And they still haven't found it?"

"No. As I say, there's apparently 500 wrecks at least down there, which hampers any search, plus all sorts of undercurrents and a thousand storms since, which could have shifted the treasure elsewhere. There have been other shipwrecks with treasure too over the years, but not on that scale."

Grandad Flint glanced at his watch.

"Now I think that'll do for today, as last night was quite hectic, and I've got a few things to attend to. We'll get down to study properly when things are sorted out and the dust has settled."

"Can we go exploring?" asked Storm.

"Your free time is yours. Just be sensible. Storm, you can sort out lunch later for you and Finn. Don't worry about me or your Mother; we're heading over to Shelley and will grab something there. Joe, one of the fishermen, has lent us another motorboat for now."

"I'm sorry." Finn looked sheepish.

"Hey, Finn. It's okay. It was exceptional circumstances. Our boat was found and towed inland by coastguards earlier today. It will be okay. Just needs a bit of repair. The engine was faulty by the way. We're just lucky none of us were killed." He shook his head. "It's not long been serviced. Very odd."

Storm looked out of the window. The sea was a shimmering ice blue and so still it looked quite eerie. The sky was a calm cobalt with a mere smattering of wispy cloud.

"Will I be okay to take the small boat out? We'll wear life jackets and not muck about."

"Of course. Finn should get back out there as soon as possible."

Storm was bursting to show Finn her discoveries. The plan was to journey to the mainland by boat and then venture back to Puffin Island through the Tunnel of Freedom. They would go swimming in the Emerald Pool Chamber through the Dome of Breath to the Creepy Cave. However, swimming may be a bad idea, after Finn almost drowned the night before, so she would see how he felt.

Storm made a huge pack lunch of chicken and ham mayo sandwiches, homemade chocolate chip cookies and crisps, to which she added a large flask of hot chocolate and bottles of water.

"I'll take my backpack, with towels, lunch and a few other bits," she said. "You lost your bag?"

"Yeah I did. But it may wash up. Had my phone on me and by some miracle it works. Have some clothes here from holidays so I'll grab my swim shorts."

"You be okay swimming in a pool, not the sea?"

"What, you mean after nearly swallowing most of the Firth of Forth?"

"Yeah and like nearly dying!"

"I'll be okay. Are we swimming at the Sporti?"

"Nah. Wait and see."

"Mysterious!" Finn raised his eyes to the ceiling. "Bit embarrassing to be honest, plus terrifying!" He shook his head in disgust. "I don't want to talk about it."

Storm decided to row across to the mainland as the sea was like a sheet of liquid glass. The oars sliced through the smooth surface, causing ripples. The sun shone down from an azure sky dotted with an array of clouds shaped like magical hills and valleys and giant eyes in the sky.

Half way out, Storm withdrew the oars, placing them in the boat. The water lapped at the edge of the vessel as she sat facing Finn.

"All good?"

"All good." Glancing back the way they'd come, he ran his fingers through his hair. "Look at it. You wouldn't believe it's the same place."

"For sure." Storm nodded.

"So different in the dark. In a storm. I was doing okay until the engine cut out. The boat was coping, massive waves though they were. But with no power, I was screwed. I kept thinking about Mum being left with me dead and my dad missing – MIA, whatever they call it....stuck with John the Psycho. I'm a good swimmer or I wouldn't have chanced it in that weather. I must have bashed my head too 'cause I don't remember half of it."

"You got a lump?"

"A bit of one." He rubbed the side of his temple. "The medic seemed to think all was okay."

"The boat flipped. Dad said it's normal not to remember stuff like that. You did what you had to in a crap situation, Finn."

"Yeah, stupid though. If your dad hadn't turned up .....!"

"You hanging with him from the Chinook! You were out of it."

"Blacked out and missed it!"

"I've never been so scared in my life. Not even at school," Storm shook her head, "felt so useless."

"You're not. I'm a bloody idiot."

Storm started rowing again. "You're not, Finn. Just desperate and panicked and God knows, I know what that feels like. Dad's involved now so he'll sort things out. He's right; you've changed a bad situation."

"Still feel like an idiot," he muttered. "Where is it we're going?"

"Bit mad, but to the mainland then back to the island. Then back again. Then back by sea. There's a couple of underwater rock pools on the west of the island I want us to have a look at."

"So going to the mainland, back to the island, then back and back again! What?" Finn shook his head laughing with confusion. "Talking in riddles."

Storm laughed. "You'll see. But you have to swear to secrecy, Finn. Even if you get tortured, you can't tell. This is like a family secret. It's massive."

"Course. I swear. Even though I have zero clue what you're on about." Finn nodded.

They moored the boat at the boathouse. "Happy memories," Storm said, glancing at Finn.

"Yeah. Returned to the scene of the crime. Like I say, it's all a big blur." He laughed.

Opening the Boathouse Cabin with the keys taken from the Keeper of Keys, Storm locked the door and walked over to the trap door. Pulling it up, she looked at Finn and raised her eyebrows.

"Secret passageway." Her eyes glinted as she passed on the top secret information with maximum drama.

"No way!"

Storm nodded, clicking locks open.

"Oh wow! How did you find this?"

"I'll fill you in on the way. There's rungs down the wall, so climb down and wait for me at the bottom." She gave Finn the head torch.

"What's down there? Is it safe?" He shone the torch down into the dark passage below. "Is this for real? Looks creepy."

"It's safe. It's a tunnel under the sea."

"Oh real safe then. Just a few thousand tons of water over our heads! No way! Like a smugglers' route?"

"Kinda, yeah."

"Where does it go? Oh my God, to the island? It leads to Puffin Island?"

"Wait and see!" Storm was enjoying the theatre. Finn's surprised reaction and excitement were what she had hoped for. Locking up the trapdoor she joined him in the dim passageway.

"So what is this place? Is it man-made?" His eyes sparkled with curiosity and the prospect of adventure.

"I think it's really old and is mostly natural caves made into a long tunnel, like, years ago. It's why it zig zags in places. You've no idea how cool it is. It leads to Puffin Island, to the lower cellar. But there's also…well you'll see. There's more going on."

It was fun sharing her secret with Finn. She felt like Storm the adventurer who had discovered a new world. How exciting it must have been for Christopher Columbus discovering America. What a buzz!

"I was getting potatoes for tea from the cellar and I saw this black round handle and trap door under one of the potato sacks. Did a search of the cellar, and found keys behind the old Puffin Island painting. They open the trapdoors to this place and other doors too. There's a door up here on the right that's locked, but the other two are like for storage, full of stores and old furniture and books." She swung the beam of light at them as they arrived.

Finn's face was a picture, with amazement stamped all over it. He started laughing. "I really must have banged my head. I feel like I'm in a Tomb Raider game or Indiana Jones movie! One minute I'm scrapping with Psycho John in Gravestone, the next I'm on a Hollywood blockbuster set."

"A Puffin Island production."

They burst out laughing.

"Yeah!"

"I know. It's mental. Feels like about a hundred years since last Friday when I got suspended from school for my hair! So much has happened."

Finn looked at her inquisitively, as he peered into the open rooms.

"This one's like an underground bedroom." He was looking in the door that housed the paintings, ornate bed and stores of food and rugs. "Someone been staying here?"

Storm shrugged her shoulders.

"Odd place for an Airbnb!"

They laughed.

"Maybe. God knows. Especially with our family."

"To do with Special Forces?"

"You know as much as me. Likely do you think?"

"Unless it's like one of those nuclear bunkers that rich people have made. Trump has one."

"Possible." Finn nodded. "So this is your old man's stuff." He pointed at the large pile of kit including diving gear. "And another bed and sheets and blankets?"

He pulled at the iron ring on the thick oak door that was firmly shut.

"Wonder what's in here." He bent trying to look and shine the torch through the key-hole at the same time. Blackness greeted him. "It's got one of those key guards things, can't see. Defo something suspicious or secret in there." He hovered, putting his ear to the wood. "You think someone's in there?"

"Don't say that, Finn. Creeps me out!"

He looked around. "We need a thin piece of metal or something to push that disc out of the way."

"We can come back to that tomorrow. It's an odd one. Can't find a key for it. It's like out of bounds." Storm shivered at the thought of strangers' eyes behind the door. Her mind returned to the split second movement of the door she thought she'd merely imagined the night before. What if Finn was right?

They stopped at the alcove that led down to the Emerald Pool Chamber.

"Where does this go?" asked Finn.

Storm lifted the large rectangular slap. Flashing the light into the hole she smiled at Finn.

"Adventure time!"

They made their way down the slate steps arriving at the man-made sealed door.

"What the hell? This is beyond bizarre!"

"You ready for this?"

"Hell yeah!"

The lock clicked open.

"Wait here a minute."

Storm lit the candles and lanterns on the rocky shelves to show off the Emerald Pool Chamber in its full splendour. The green water gleamed invitingly in the candlelight.

Storm went to the doorway to collect Finn. Shutting the door, she led him into the chamber.

"Oh wow!" Aghast, he looked around, taking in his mysterious surroundings. "It's easily the size of a proper swimming pool." He crouched and felt the water. "Not heated though!" He grinned.

Storm handed him the torch to look around while she unpacked their swimwear, thick towels, blankets and lunch.

"Aw, food!" said Finn excitedly.

"I'm not sure what you're more excited about," Storm laughed, pouring them both a mug of hot chocolate from the large flask.

"I'm speechless to be honest, Storm." He sat down next to Storm. She passed him a chicken ham and mayo sandwich from the vast stack she'd made.

"I only discovered this, Thursday."

"No way. It's awesome. What's that archway down at the end of the pool? It looks like a hole in the rock."

"It leads somewhere else into another cave. I was gonna say we'd swim through it, but after yesterday we don't want a repeat."

"What you mean repeat?"

"Well I swam through the arch. Had Dad's headtorch on from his stuff. There's this dome-like bit, an air pocket in the middle I've named "The Dome of Breath". Took a massive breath and swam on about two meters then upwards. Thought it would be the same depth as this pool. I've called this "The Emerald Pool Chamber.""

Finn took another sandwich, nodding with approval.

"Did you bring any water?"

Storm handed him a bottle.

"Thanks. Go on."

"Well it happens it's deeper and the water level is higher. Put it this way: you're not the only one that nearly drowned. I got about half way up and ran out of breath."

Finn stopped chewing.

"Was trying to propel myself up with my arms. Then…." Storm shuddered.

"I know." Finn patted her on the arm.

"There's more.   It wasn't just that I couldn't breathe. I saw this dark shape and huge crusted eyes. It frightened the life out of me and I panicked. The eyes were old port holes. It's an old wreck sitting in the water like a ghost ship."

"Bloody hell!"

"Adrenalin got me to the surface. I was totally out of air and my lungs were painful and burning. I was in this creepy place gasping like a captured fish in a trawler net, coughing and choking, desperate for air."

"Totally terrifying!" Finn nodded.

"So I kinda know how you feel Finn. Last night you were lifeless, then choking, bringing up sea water from your lungs and gasping for air. It was similar for me, only I was in the first stage of about to pass out… whereas you actually did pass out and… nearly went the whole way and died."

"Jeez when you say it like that."

They both started laughing.

"Plus I was also an idiot. Fancy swimming somewhere strange with a lung full of air. I didn't know the depth or where I was going. So I get how you feel about taking the boat, flipping it and nearly drowning."

"So you admit I am an idiot then," he laughed, then grimaced. "And being rescued by the SAS and worse, my dad's best mate! How embarrassing is that! None of them are gonna think I'm a chip off the old block."

"Took guts, Finn, too."

"Was stupid. But look at you. Wow my little cousin's turned into

Lara Croft!"

Storm hit him with her towel.

Finn drank down his hot chocolate.

"What a pair. Both nearly drowned a mere day apart. But…"

"But now Locke and Swift have turned into intrepid adventurers. Discovered an underworld of tunnels and shipwrecks and a creepy cave next-door!" Storm interjected dramatically.

Finn started laughing a deep throaty sound that echoed around the Emerald Pool Chamber. Storm joined in and they laughed until tears were streaming down their faces.

"Oh my sides." Finn wiped his eyes.

"Mine too."

Storm passed him a packet of crisps and they sat munching, viewing the pool, both deep in thought.

"You know, I think we need to go through your old man's kit. I did a bit of diving last year before everything went south. Dad took me just before he went MIA. Just these small oxygen tanks you clip on to your belt. They hold enough air for about an hour, maybe a bit more. The tanks Dad and I used were military issue, so figure there may be some in the pile. Dad being Dad showed me all the tech stuff too, maintenance, refill, etc." He took the cookie offered. "Everything we do, it's like: 'one day you might need to know this' lesson." Finn put on a deeper voice to imitate his Father Josh.

"I know exactly what you mean. Where do you think he is?"

"I know he's not dead." He put his clenched fist to his chest. "Most think so but this is what they're trained for: to disappear." He shook his head. "Nah. He'll turn up."

"So what's the plan?" asked Storm. "Shall we go check out the kit? Then come back here and try it out in the pool?"

"Yeah, make sure it works. Don't want to drown twice in one week."

"Last night made you feel different?" Storm asked.

"Defo." Finn glanced at Storm. "I feel older somehow, as if someone's put a light on in a dim room. Can't explain it."

Storm nodded and jumped to her feet.

"Me too. Exactly. Let's go."

They made their way to where the pile of kit lay in one of the open rooms.

"Yes! This is it." In one of the crates was diving equipment. Among it was scuba diving gear and the small oxygen cylinders Finn had mentioned.

"We can use them for the rock pools later."

Finn nodded. He was checking dates, and refill entries on the side of the cylinders. He pointed at larger tanks.

"Cool for refill."

"Perfect."

Gathering up what they needed, they made their way back to the chamber.

"You think Pop's would have put electric down here with all this," said Finn. "Bit of light. Heating maybe."

"Yeah it's pretty cold." Storm laughed.

"Just a bit."

"Do you think it floods in the winter? The door to the pool chamber has a seal." Storm had been wondering what the seal was for.

"Hmm, possibly. If so there must be a gap somewhere to let in sea water. It may be just a precaution, because of the rooms being used for storage."

"Yeah sounds right. There could be a route out to the sea though otherwise the pools would stagnate. I dunno I'm just guessing."

They changed into their swimwear, under towels.

"My theory is that the Creepy Cave was just a cave and inlet. The Ghost Ship was driven in there during bad weather, dashed on the rocks and later sank. It's mostly under water. At some point after that, there was a rock fall that sealed the entrance, trapping it in there for eternity."

"A watery tomb. That makes a lot of sense." Finn was assembling the diving equipment. "Jeez hope there's no skeletons down there."

"Finn, for God sake. I never thought of that!"

"Mwah ha ha ha ha! It is indeed a Ghost Ship full of the trapped spirits of ancient sailors." Finn put on an evil laugh.

"Finn shut up!" Storm chucked his jumper at him.

He picked Storm up like a baby and dumped her into the pool. Jumping in, he shone the underwater torch around the pool.

"You wait!" She screamed, resurfacing.

Finn laughed; his long eyelashes were stuck together, and his eyes twinkled with fun. He looked like his old self, not the miserable quiet boy he'd become.

Finn grabbed the equipment.

"I'll test it out in here. Then you have a go."

"Okay!" Storm swam around the pool, duck-diving near the archway entrance to the Creepy Cave. She tried sitting on the bottom on the white sand, holding her breath for as long as possible. Her heel grazed against something hard. Resurfacing, she took a breath and dived down once more. Holding onto the side of the arch, she dug into the sand with her fingers, plucking out a deep red stone about the size of two thumb nails that looked like shiny sea glass.

Swimming over to Finn, he gave her the thumbs up. The equipment was in full working order.

Signalling him over to the side of the pool, she showed him her findings. At six foot one, Finn could stand on the bottom, whereas Storm had to hold on to the side of the pool.

"What do you think this is? Sea glass?" Sea glass was old glass smoothed by the movement of the tide over the ages.

Finn held it up near the light of the lantern.

"No idea. Could be. It's a weird shape for that though. Quite thick." He looked at Storm. "Maybe it's part of Charles 1 lost treasure!" He put on an English upper class accent. "It's a ruby fallen out of the handle of his silver serving spoon."

"Idiot!" she said laughing. "Anyway I thought he was Scottish."

"Brought up in France. I think he was exiled." Finn said, attempting to sound knowledgeable.

"That was Bonnie Prince Charlie. Is that the same as Charles 1?" Storm frowned.

"No clue. That's one for Grandad Flint's next history lesson. A good follow on."

"Thinking about it. We may find quite a few things on our explorations. We should find somewhere to hide our collection. Finn and Storm's secret stash."

"Maybe that's what's hidden in the secret locked room."

"Nah! That's far-fetched."

"And all this isn't!" Storm glared at him.

"Okay. Point taken. Stroppy!"

"We don't know who or what's behind that door; that's the thing."

"Truth. Right I'll show you how to use this. Then we'll warm up a bit. Then off to The Creepy Cave!"

CHAPTER 12
The Ghost Ship

Under Finn's instruction, Storm practised using the diving equipment. When they were both satisfied that they knew what they were doing and it was working properly, Finn went back to the kit room and made sure the tanks were full.

"You've already been to The Creepy Cave, so you go first... same route, until I get my bearings."

A buzzing sound echoing through the rock walls.

"Oh, no way!" Finn threw back his head and roared with laughter. "A signal down here! Oh this just gets better."

Storm's phone was vibrating. It was a message from her dad saying that Aunt Molly and he were stopping off in Newcastle for the night as they needed to talk, and would be back first thing and to stay out of mischief until they got back. And Mum says dinner is at 18:00 sharp. There was also a message from Storm's mum with virtually the same content.

"It's Dad. He's with your mum. Did you get a text? Dinner's at six."

"Yeah from Mum." Finn put his phone back in the rucksack. "She's texted me about five times saying sorry and how relieved she is I'm okay. I said I'm cool with it."

"Prob feels bad about the Psycho John thing."

Finn shook his head.

"She just went a bit mental for a bit I guess."

"Happens. Seems to run in the family. Ready?"

"Yeah good to go?"

"I'll go first?"

"Storm Swift the new Lara Croft leads the way into the murky depths of the haunted cavern." Finn gestured to the pool.

"Shut up Finn!"

"I can go first if you're scared. Only I might go the wrong way. Straight into the jaws of the monster."

"I'll go first and let's see how brave you are when you see it. It's freaky plus I did nearly drown!"

"Same! I nearly drowned too. But I'm standing here in the water," Finn said indignantly.

Storm grinned, and inserting the mouth piece, she switched on air and placed goggles over her eyes. Flicking the head torch on she disappeared into the darkness of the archway that led to The Creepy Chamber. Pausing, she pointed at the Dome of Breath in the middle of the two archways before swimming down the small tunnel that ran into the seaweed laced waters surrounding the wreck.

As planned she swam upwards, leading the way past the encrusted port holes of the Ghost Ship. Up, up to the surface. It seemed like miles, and Storm was amazed she'd managed the route without the aid of an oxygen tank.

Breaking the surface she grabbed the rock ledge and shone the torchlight around the cavern, waiting for Finn. The top of the ship just poked out from its place of rest.

Finn emerged.

"You okay?" Storm asked.

"Yeah. See what you mean though." He looked at Storm with renewed respect. "You did this on your own and without air too. You're right too. It is bloody creepy. Just suddenly looms out of a weird gloom." He shuddered.

"As you said: Lara Croft, tomb raider, move over!"

Finn laughed.

"I'm glad we have these though!" He tapped his air tank with his finger.

"Too much after last night?"

"Nah, I'm good. Just made me jump. And I knew it was there. God knows how you felt."

"Spooked me! Believe me. Let's check out around the wreck then have a look inside if we can."

Diving back down, they made their way along the starboard left side of the ship, shining the torch light around at their underwater surroundings. A garden of seaweed, shells, and rockery sprouting unknown plants, waved at them with lime green and sludge brown leaves. The archway entrance into the chamber shone in the distance, and the seabed was littered with huge black boulders that had randomly fallen. It seemed Storm's theory about the rock fall entombing the Ghost Ship was right.

The vessel was covered in a grey coral, and the tail end looked like a massive gutted fish. The damage was incredible. Just a hollow at the stern, the back of the ship, as most of the deck had rotted or been eaten away. Swimming up to the bow at the front area, it appeared more intact. They hovered over the deck, part of which was above the water. Storm remembered her dream about the ornate chair, table and emerald mermaid. If that creature showed up with its peculiar glinting eyes, it would finish her off for sure. That was one monster that could stay in her head.

Swimming down further through broken decking and rotted stairwells into the inwards of the ghost ship was eerie. Storm suspected that the wreck had been explored many times before by Grandad Flint and probably the rest of the family. She doubted they would find anything of value, but just the experience of exploring an ancient wreck for the first time was quite a buzz. Descending further, they came to a thick wooden doorway. The door swung open easily. It must have been the captain's quarters.

Swinging the light around, there was a pile of old sticks buried under heaps of sand and broken shells, which may have once been a table and chairs. Storm swam down to the floor level and disturbed the dirt with her hand in the hope something had been buried there. Her fingers touched on something cold, and digging frantically, she unearthed a common piece of black rock. Chucking it to the floor, she swam near the old round windows. Embedded in the wood was a piece of metal. Pulling it out, it appeared to be an old candle holder. She pointed excitedly to Finn who swooped down to collect it.

There were old cupboards but they needed a more extensive search in order to find anything of interest. However, Storm was thrilled; if she'd managed to discover the candle holder, after all this time, what else was hidden under the rubble? Plus, they hadn't explored the rest of the ship yet, but Finn was tapping his watch and pointing upwards. He was worried that they would run out of air.

Finn swam up and then along the port side to the right of the wreck checking out the depth of the ship. Swimming down across the sea bed, he suddenly stopped and waved frantically to Storm to hurry over. Shining the beam through the water at the cavern wall, it displayed another archway. This one was on the seaward side of the cave where the entrance would once have been, before it became a sealed chamber.

Storm joined Finn, holding on to a black boulder to stop her body from floating upwards. They stared incredulously! There was a manufactured door, smaller but of similar design to the one that led into the Emerald Pool Chamber. The mystery thickened, for there were no key holes in this door; instead there was a panel containing a number code locking mechanism.

Moving nearer; Finn and Storm exchanged glances. The numbers were from one to twenty six! Crack that code and they would discover what lay beyond the door. What was the purpose of it? It was now clear that this underground world was more than utilising old chambers for leisure, storage and convenience. It was mixed up with the work of Grandad Flint, Flint Jnr and maybe even Finn's father Josh.

Finn tapped his watch. They had mere minutes of air left and swam at speed back to the archway that led to the Emerald Pool Chamber. Re-surfacing in the friendly green water, they removed their diving equipment, shivering and shaking, teeth chattering with cold. Wrapping their freezing bodies in large bath sheets and blankets, Storm handed Finn a steaming cup of hot chocolate. They both took frantic sips, enjoying the reviving sweetness of the sugar and heat sensation as the liquid stole downwards warming their bodies.

"Wow." Rejuvenated, Finn spoke first.

"I know." Storm rubbed the water from her hair with a towel.

"That was like epic. Can't even process it." He shook his head.

"Mad!" Storm was also speechless.

"Totally! Where d'you think that door leads?"

Storm handed Finn a ham and cheese sandwich, biting into one herself. Taking out a blanket, she placed it over them for additional warmth. The water was cold and they'd stayed submerged longer than sensible. It had been so fascinating they'd lost track of time.

"Logically, it's a sea access. For what purpose, God knows."

"You know, Finn, when I found this place, I knew it was bizarre, but all this!"

The candle holder, tarnished and encrusted with coral, sat in the chamber.

"What a find. Think it will survive a clean?" Storm looked at it in wonder. "Must be ancient."

"Could try it. Mum soaks silver in hot washing up liquid, so worth a go," suggested Finn, happily accepting a large chocolate cookie from the bag, dunking it in his hot chocolate. "Might be brass or maybe even metal. We'll know when it's clean. You like puzzles?"

"Haven't done one for ages but can give it a go." Storm laughed.

"What you thinking so far?" He took another cookie.

"Give away. The numbers."

Finn nodded.

"Detective Swift and Locke have deduced that the one to twenty six numbers can mean only one thing…!" Finn announced dramatically.

"It's a word!" They said in unison, chuckling.

"We used to do that all the time as kids." Storm said. "Talk parrot fashion."

"Yeah people thought we were twins," Finn joked.

"Can happen. I think I read about a white woman who had twins and one baby was white and the other that was black."

"Just hope her husband wasn't white then," Finn laughed.

"Can you imagine the shit storm that would cause! One word or two?" Storm rummaged in the bag and handed Finn a bottle of water. "Couldn't see a space button, so maybe one. But what word, could be anything!"

"Further, find the word and then we have to decrypt it and work out the number code, as it's a numbers panel."

"Yeah, assuming it is a word." Finn drained most of the bottle of water. "Twenty six letters in the alphabet. Unless it's a trick."

"Let's break down what we know." Storm glanced at her phone. "Five pm. Dinner's at six. We'll sit somewhere warm and brainstorm. We can sit in the Zen room with the fire on. "

"Sounds good to me. Swear my body's gonna stay numb for eternity. Not sure I'll ever feel my feet again. Let's get this lot packed away."

After a dinner of hot steaming shepherd's pie with broccoli which they ate in the dining room with Grandad Flint and Storm's mother, Finn and Storm sat in the Zen room watching the heaving gun metal waves through the giant clear glass windows. A small fire burned in the wood burner. The candle holder was immersed in a bucket of hot soapy water in the bathroom to soak overnight along with the red stone Storm had discovered earlier that day.

The wind began to howl as they sat on beanbags warm and snug. Marmite was asleep on the fluffy red blanket, and Marmalade had sneaked in undetected by his sleeping brother who always hissed at him, and snuggled in front of the flickering orange fire. Pad and pencil in hand, Storm and Finn began the process of elimination. What could the mysterious code be?

CHAPTER 13

The Puzzle

Torrential rain fell the next day and it was forecast all week.

Storm and Finn had a maths lesson in the morning, which consisted of times tables, fractions and a mixture of sums.

"And…!" Grandad Flint dramatically announced, "you have homework! Robert Louis Stevenson's *Treasure Island*. Read chapter one to three, and we'll discuss next lesson. A follow-on from our history lesson about the treasure discovered in the Forth."

Storm almost visibly jumped when he declared the title of the book. *Treasure Island* was the book that belonged to her dad. It was the one she'd picked up from the chest. What a weird coincidence.

"Can find it on kindle, think it's free. But we definitely have copies around somewhere," he added vaguely, gesturing at the bookcase lining the left wall packed with a variety of books, before disappearing into his study.

Finn's mother and Flint Jnr were due back at tea time and so they had the afternoon to work further on the puzzle. So far they hadn't got very far. They returned to the Zen room and Storm relit the fire.

"Let's assume the codes have been set by either Grandad Flint or Uncle Flint Jnr. Could be Puffin Island? Lily Swift, Storm Swift? SAS or Finn Locke, wonderful nephew?" enthused Finn.

"All quite obvious," Storm laughed. "Apart from the last. Okay, so say it's Puffin Island. I think how code works is that the P would be letter 1 instead of A being letter 1 and you work out the code from there."

"What? So normally you'd have A=1 B=2 C=3 but in code it would be like P=1, then U would be letter number 6?"

"Yeah, exactly. So not only have we gotta work out the word; we've gotta work this out too. How are we supposed to do this?"

"We're not. That's the point."

"This is giving me a major headache."

"Same. It's like impossible. Shall I make us bacon and egg sandwiches, then go rummage through the storage rooms?"

"Yeah, sounds good. I would help, but cooking's not quite my thing, usually end up setting off the fire alarms."

"Sure, Finn." Storm stood up. "Like I've never heard that one before."

"Lunch, then a major delve," Finn grinned, "never know what we'll find. Maybe some mysterious clue. Have you got a thin piece of metal? I'm thinking, look through the keyhole of the locked room."

"You're obsessed with that door."

"Just wanna know what's inside."

"Got a skewer type thing for roasting marshmallows in the drawer in the kitchen."

Storm cooked lunch and returned to the Zen room with hot bacon and egg sandwiches and tea.

"Nice." Finn devoured the sandwich with enjoyment. "You're not a bad cook you know, cuz."

"I get plenty of practice!"

CHAPTER 14
Rage and Discovery

Venturing down to the cellar, they vanished once more into the depth of Puffin Island. Standing in the ornate storage room, Finn lit eight lanterns illuminating the room so that they could see properly instead of peering through layers of sinister shadows.

He stood frowning at the locked door.

"And you say the key for this is nowhere to be found."

"Nah, I looked. The other keys are with the Keeper of Keys: the old Puffin Island Painting. This one isn't. If it's important, it's maybe locked away in Grandad Flint's safe in his study."

"And we can't go in there?"

"No. No way. It's clearly out of bounds. I've never even been in there and he locks the door when he leaves."

"Secretive." Finn looked at the door. "I've been thinking."

"Terrifying!"

"Haha! Mum and Dad had a row, one of many before they split up, when we were still here in Shelley. But this particular row was about his job. Not about him being away, more to do with danger. Only heard bits but something about him getting mixed up with some gang on purpose. Then doors banged. The usual. After that, they split. He disappeared; Mum started seeing a lot of John the Psycho. Then hell reigned and we moved to Gravestone."

"What a name for a town. And you're thinking?"

"Town's something to do with the Black Death years ago. Some plague. What I'm thinking is, what if your dad is hiding my dad in there?"

Storm looked at him and then at their surroundings.

"What for six months? Down here! Why would he?"

"This place is littered with strange doors, passageways and chambers!" Finn raised his voice. "Leads down to ...." He pointed down the tunnel towards mainland Shelley. "It leads to the mainland. He pretty much has freedom to go wherever and come back here." He picked up a tin of peas and absentmindedly examined the sell-by date. "What if he's in trouble or in danger and in hiding?"

Storm looked at Finn with concern. "Finn, he may be dead. He wouldn't let you just wonder." Storm said quietly. "You have to accept it's possible."

"I don't!" He yelled slamming the peas down on the shelf. "It's his job, isn't it, to disappear?"

"I know. I'm just saying! But I hear you and, it did occur to me too, not so much about Uncle Josh, but Dad hiding people down here maybe, judging by all the stuff stored here. But it's a bizarre thought."

"All this is... It's doing my head in."

Storm raised her eyebrows enquiringly.

"Him. Dad. Not knowing." Finn clarified.

Storm sat down on the sturdy chest stuffed with her dad's old books.

"The night of the storm I came racing down here on my way to the boathouse. I was convinced you were there, maybe sheltering, waiting for the morning."

Finn snorted.

"As if I'm ever that sensible!"

"I swear I saw that door," Storm pointed at the thick oak door, "moving, closing. It was a microsecond of movement." Taking a deep breath, Storm relayed the overheard conversation between Grandad Flint and her dad the day before. "Seems they're worried about some people, that our dad's may have caused problems for."

Finn stared at Storm.

"Well that makes it even more likely! All the answers are behind that door!" He inserted the marshmallow skewer into the lock wiggling it. Shining the torch at the same time, he sighed with frustration. "Still can't see anything." He kicked the door impatiently. "Let's just have a look through some stuff."

Flicking through old paintings, mainly of the island and various seabirds, Storm watched Finn picking up every jar and tin on the shelves and looking beneath. He was on a mission.

"You okay Finn?"

He seemed really wound up.

"I just hate not knowing Storm!" he yelled. "Not knowing about my dad and what's happened to him! If he's dead. I just want to know! I'm like a puppet."

"What do you mean?"

"I have no say in anything. Just told what to do. Like being shipped off down south. I wasn't even allowed to question it, even though it's my life too and I bloody hated it there. I had to stay and try and like that lazy psycho! Like now, where am I gonna be made to live next? With Mum's next idiot. Who's he gonna be? A serial killer?" He clenched his fists. "I just feel so so angry, pissed off, and like smashing everything to pieces most of the time!"

"Hardly surprising. It's been shit for you, Finn."

"I hate being this age. I'm like virtually an adult but treated like a child! And that John! God I hated him so much!" He paced up and down on the Turkish rug. "All I could hear after we moved down, was Mum crying and him shouting at her about how pathetic she was. He's a dirty drunk. Glued to the sofa day after day with his beer cans, whisky bottles. Sat on his fat lazy arse. He's like the opposite of my dad. Why would she even like him? I was mad at Mum for being so dumb, and smashing our family to bits."

He ran his fingers through his dark hair.

"I hate! hate that psycho!" He balled his fish smacking it into his palm. "I just lost it. He was on the whisky and pick, picking at her. I could hear him from my shitty room in this awful grey house with paper thin walls." He paused taking a breath. "I just ran down the hall and burst into the living room screaming: 'Shut up, just shut up!' and then swore at him. Once I started ranting I couldn't stop. Mum was sobbing on the sofa, and the next minute he threw a punch and hit my cheekbone. She was like screaming. I threw him on the floor and we were rolling around kicking and punching. I punched him in the face and ran, locking myself in the bathroom. Mum eventually calmed him down."

"I love her. I do, but I can't. I just can't. I had to go. I went to my room that's on the ground floor. Packed as much as I could, nicked a bunch of money from John's wallet he'd left on the sofa and left." He wiped his nose on his sleeve. "Had to. If I'd stayed I'd have died for sure or been done for murder. It was hell."

"Aw, Finn, sounds grim."

He nodded. "Least she's away from him for a bit, and with your dad. He might talk some sense into her. I don't want to live away from her, but I'm not ever going back. I'd rather die."

"Hey," Storm tugged his sleeve. "You won't have to."

He looked down at her and smiled looking embarrassed.

"Dunno where all that came from."

"You've had a really shitty time, Finn. I get it. Really I do. I felt like that with school. I know it's different, but that feeling of having to do what everyone else thought best. No one listening to me and acting like I'm making shit up all the time, not being in control of your own life."

Finn nodded.

"Finn, it's so not cool to keep all that crap inside you. Really. It's good to get it out. I know. I went to this counsellor Tess, to do with anxiety. Thought it was a stupid idea but it actually made a difference, felt better, lighter in here." Storm put her palm on her chest.

"Okay, Counsellor Storm. Look at you all mature." He laughed. "But I actually do feel better. How weird is that. Right, drama done! Let's get on. "

Storm stood up.

"So the homework, *Treasure Island*, I guess is a perfect follow from the history lesson, plus we live on an island. I just have a feeling…"

"You live on an island. I am a homeless person," said Finn morosely

"Jeez such drama Finn! Grandad Flint is your Grandad too. We'll sort it out."

"I'll speak to Mum about staying here on the island, and to Pops," said Finn hopefully.

Storm opened the chest she'd been sitting on.

"Finn, here's the copy of *Treasure Island*. My dad's old school book. I came across it the first day I discovered this place."

She handed it to Finn, who flicked through it.

"It must be really old. Pages are like gold edged."

"Looks ancient." said Storm. "It's got his name on it."

Finn turned the page. "People always used to write in books. Pop's said it was kinda like a thing, to give each other a book and a message written in it. Here Storm, look at this." Turning the next page he saw scribbling on the old parchment in dark blue ink pen. The writing was large and looping in the same handwriting as Flint Jnr's name.

1:

"What the actual...This must be it!" Storm said taking the book and looking at it incredulously. They looked at each other excitedly.

"Seems a bit easy?" Finn frowned, narrowing his eyes suspiciously.

"Only easy because we have the book though." Storm's phone buzzed. "Truth. If you hadn't seen this encryption we'd still be trying to solve this puzzle when we're ninety. There's no way on God's earth that code was ever gonna be cracked by us." She pulled her phone from her pocket. "Damn, it's tea time. Finn, your mum's home!"

They returned to the Light House to the smell of gammon steaks with pineapple, broccoli and new potatoes in butter cooking for dinner. Entering the dining room, Finn was engulfed with hugs from Molly, who sobbed into his shoulder.

"I'll make it up to you. I promise. I'm so sorry."

Sitting down to eat, Storm's father winked at her, and relief surged through her. She had a feeling that from then onwards, things were going to get dramatically better for both Finn and herself.

***

The following week was busy, packed full of lessons, homework and family time. Molly had decided to stay for the time being and sort things out with Finn. She had finished the relationship with John the Psycho the day Flint Jnr had gone to collect her. Grandad Flint sent a team to collect up their belongings and store them nearby in an industrial storage facility near Edinburgh. Storm and Lily spent a few days with her dad   before he headed back up to Shetland. There was simply no time to try out the code on the locked archway door. The following Saturday, Lily, Molly and Grandad Flint were going into Edinburgh for a hospital check up on Grandad Flint's broken ankle. Finn and Storm finally had a clear day to try out the code.

CHAPTER 15
The Code and Intruders

"Bletchley Park code breakers in action." Finn threw some diving equipment at Storm. They were in the Emerald Pool Chamber.

Storm laughed.

"They broke the German 'Nazis' Codes during the war! Using an Enigma machine." He continued.

"I know that!" Storm shook her head. "Just cause you paid attention in one history lesson ever."

"Remembering the numbers is gonna be the tricky bit."

"I'll remember 'Treasure', you 'Island'."

"Good thinking."

They sat chanting the numbers, imprinting them into their brains. Plunging into the cool waters, they swam through the Archway, the Dome of Breath and along the short tunnel into the Creepy Cave. This time they headed straight for the Coded Sea Arch. They'd decided that the code must be the numbers to TREASUREISLAND as one word, so Storm punched in her numbers, then Finn his. No click. No movement. Storm pointed upwards and they broke the surface.

"What the..." began Finn.

"I don't get it. Unless..."

"What?"

"Well." Storm began excitedly. "Remember in Dad's book it's written as 1 and 2. It clearly separates the words."

"So we just put in Treasure?"

"No clue, but let's try."

Diving down to the door, Storm punched in 1-25-12-8-26-2-25-12, the encrypted code for TREASURE, and this time they paused. A clunk. Finn pulled the door open. Beyond it was another door with the same panel. Finn punched in: 16-26-19-8-21-11, the code for ISLAND, and paused. Nothing. They hovered in the watery rock passageway.

Storm looked behind the first door. It was thick grey and made of some sort of rust proof metal. There was another keypad for re-entry. It seemed this door may need to be closed for the other to open. It was a risk. If the island code for the second door was wrong, and the re-entry code was different to the ones they had worked out, then they would be trapped, entombed there for-ever alongside the Ghost Ship, eventually drowning when their air ran out.

She looked at Finn through her goggles. He seemed to know what she was thinking and nodded, closing the first door. As it clicked shut he punched the island code into the second door. A resounding clunk. Relief flooded, as the outer door swung open. Swimming through, they closed the door behind them. Torch light revealed that they were in a round rocky well. It seemed the only route was upwards. Swimming strongly, they surfaced in sea water in the underwater rock pool to the west side of the island.

The strong scent of sea salt and the shrill chatter of gulls hit their senses. Bright sunlight replaced the dimness of the underworld. The sea was a deep dark blue, an innocent blanket covering the mysteries below.

Puffin Island had an underwater entrance! As well as an underground land entrance via the boathouse cabin, all protected by keys, locks and codes. It was indeed a mystery to uncover. Finn and Storm had no time to enjoy their discovery however, as a strange white yacht, glossy and elegant had appeared in the bay anchored further up the Firth of Forth. A black motorboat appeared from the starboard side, zooming out over the water, casting a trail   of white froth on the navy sea. It was heading towards Puffin Island. Finn and Storm looked at each other in alarm.

Puffin Island was private property, and trespassers had no right to be there. The boat was heading for the stretch of sandy beach just along from where they were hidden.

"Drug dealers?" Finn whispered.

"Maybe! Shouldn't be here; that's for sure," Storm hissed back. "Who knows?"

The boat cut its engine and sat in the shallows water lapping up against the bow. Male voices replaced the drone.

"Sound foreign." Storm said.

"Yeah, for sure."

One of the men was pointing to the cave at the end of the beach that Storm had identified weeks before when she'd been out for a walk. A pile of boulders were stacked up the cliff face. The small man in the motorboat appeared to be arguing with one of the others. A taller man shouted something to him and he jumped out into the water, gesturing at the two other men standing idle. They were dressed in black combats and t-shirts with head coverings.

The man trudged up the beach, his shoulders rounded and fists clenched. He seemed angry. Climbing up two of the boulders, he began carelessly hauling at the middle boulder in temper. The other men stood watching, calling what appeared to be instructions. The boulder he was tugging made a grating noise as it came away from the pile.

Storm and Finn looked at each other incredulously, watching the inevitable course of events unfold. Removing the central rock caused an avalanche. Rocks bounced and cascaded, bashing the man in the face. Shrieking, he fell backwards, crashing onto the sand as falling rocks pelted him, the last but largest boulder smashing him hard on the leg. He screamed, wailing loudly in pain.

Finn and Storm gasped in shock from their hiding place.

"Totally moronic." Finn whispered to Storm.

"I have no words."

The tall man was yelling orders in a strange language, clearly furious. The other two men scrambled out of the boat in haste. Throwing off rocks they uncovered the battered man. Picking him up by the legs and arm, they roughly carried him, shouting ,back to the boat. Returning to the cave, they tried replacing the rocks, leaving the larger boulders. Their mission was a clear fail, and the boat turned and sped away back in the direction of the yacht.

Sinking further down into the bottomless rockpool, Finn and Storm watched, taking furtive glances over the top of the grey rocks. The engine of the yacht started up and the boat moved away up the Firth of Forth.

"Reckon they'll be back?" Finn asked quietly watching the boat disappearing.

"Defo. I'm frozen." Storm's teeth were chattering.

"We need to get out of this water. Let's head back, have some food and make a plan," said Finn.

"Sounds good to me".

Diving down to the bottom of the well, Finn punched the TREASURE code back into the panel on the door. Nothing happened. Storm and Finn looked at each other in horror. He tried again. Nothing. They swam back up and resurfaced in the underwater rock pool.

"What the actual...!"

"You're sure you put it in right."

"One hundred percent."

"Our fingers are freezing. I'm sure I've got brain freeze starting." Storm duck dived down again.

TREASURE she punched in the number code. Nothing. In desperation she punched in the number code for ISLAND as Finn joined her. A loud clunk. Thank God. Swimming into the Dome of Breath 2, they pulled the door shut and punched in the TREASURE number. Again a loud clunk and the door opened into the Creepy Cave.

Even the sinister Ghost Ship looked inviting and friendly, after what they just witnessed. They swam back through the arches into the Emerald Pool Chamber, clambering quickly out of the water, wrapping their ice cold bodies in thick towels and blankets.

Storm tried pouring out hot chocolate, but her hands were shaking too much.

"I'll do it." Finn took over and poured out two mugs of steaming brown liquid.

"That's so nice. I feel like I'm on slow thaw." said Storm, after taking a gulp.

Finn handed her a pair of fluffy socks out of the black rucksack.

"I packed these for us. After last time, took about two days for my feet to warm up."

"Oh my God, well done." They put on the black socks enjoying the warmth.

"Do you think that guy's dead?" Finn downed his hot chocolate and poured them both another.

Storm shook her head. "Nah, not with the noise he was making. Leg's mashed up pretty bad I'd imagine."

"What's in the fat flask?"

"Tomato soup."

"No way. You're an absolute genius."

Pouring hot tomato soup into plastic mugs, they dunked their cheese sandwiches enjoying the delicious and satisfying flavour.

"But how stupid, I mean really! Who like pulls the middle

boulder!" said Storm scornfully.

"I know really! Like something out of a gangster spoof!"

They laughed.

"Seriously though, what were they doing here? Looking for something or smuggling or what?"

"You don't think they're the gang your dad and Pops were talking about, do you?"

"Crossed my mind."

"Looking for my dad?"

"Who knows, Finn. And the doors heading back. Dunno which was scarier, the men in black landing here on our home or being stuck in the freezing well unable to get back in."

"TREASURE ISLAND on the way out. ISLAND TREASURE on the way in! As if it's not hard enough remembering the numbers, reversing them in the first stages of hypothermia is majorly complicated!" Finn grumbled.

"Madness."

"Totally. Let's pack up and go warm up. Then we'll grab some gear and set up a look out."

"Zen room's ideal."

"Yeah with lights out. Can't be seen. I think they're watching the island."

"How do you mean?" Storm shuddered involuntarily.

"Seeing who's coming and going. Maybe seen Pops, and Aunt Lily heading out, and your dad yesterday. They may not even know about us though. You use the tunnel."

"They must know about us, Finn. We took the boat out today. As far as they're concerned, the island is empty. What if they're looking for the tunnel and think the entrance is in that cave? What if the secret's been leaked?" Storm said in alarm.

"Or they don't know about the tunnel but do know that the island is littered with deep caves. They may think he's hiding in one of them!"

"One thing's for sure, Finn. We need to be careful from now on, and we should tell Grandad Flint and Mum for sure."

Finn nodded.

They tidied away the diving gear. Relocking all the doors, they headed back along the tunnel to the boat house. Finn glared at the locked door as he passed it.

"If you're in there, Dad, they're looking for you! " He kicked the door angrily. "Your son and niece have seen them!"

Storm looked at Finn. His obsession was growing by the day. Convinced that his dad was behind the door, everyday occurrences confirmed this in his mind. He was getting to the point now where he was beginning to resent him for not revealing he was there and confiding in Finn. And yet there was no evidence that he was actually on the island or alive. Storm just hoped that Finn was right because if it turned out his dad was indeed dead after all, she feared he may be enveloped by madness.

CHAPTER 16

The Storm

Arriving back at the boat house, Storm's phone pinged. She had five missed calls from her mother.

"Siri. Call Mum Swift."

"Calling Mum Swift. Home." The phone began to ring and it was answered almost immediately.

"Hi Storm. Where have you been?"

"Swimming."

"Pop's ankles been playing up as you know. Dr Battle at the hospital says it's not healing properly. Something to do with it being set incorrectly. He's got to have a small op, and they want to do it this afternoon. We want to stay in Edinburgh. I can call Aunty Clare to come over."

Aunty Clare was Lily's hippy friend from Shelley Village who stank of lavender and weed.

"Is Pops okay?"

"He's fine and told us to go home; but we'd rather stay. Weather forecast's awful too. Shall I call Clare?"

"No. We'll be fine Mum, really. It's not like I'm on my own. Finn's here. He's like six foot."

"Be fine, Aunty Lily." Finn called. "I'll look after her."

Storm glared at him.

"Yes that's why I'm not so worried." Lily said.

"I'll look after Finn," Storm said, making a point. "Give Pops our love and let us know how the op goes. Dad know?"

"He'll only worry, so no. I'll tell him after. Be careful and stay indoors."

After the phone call, Finn and Storm looked at each other.

"No telling about intruders now." Finn said looking out over the ocean.

"Do you think I should have?" asked Storm anxiously. "I wasn't sure what to do."

"They'd have come back, and Pops would be fretting. There's not a great deal to tell at the moment. We'll keep a look out."

Mother Nature had wiped the baby blue sky with light fluffy clouds from the canvas, replacing it instead with dark grey streaks of silver and black. The navy sea had suffered the same fate and was now a dolphin grey with white tips.

"We better get back. Looks like a storm's brewing." Storm looked anxiously up at the sky.

They moored the boat tightly at Puffin Island quay as rain drops began to fall. Sitting in the Zen room with the lights off, they looked out over the bay through binoculars.

"You keep watch. I'll make us some food."

Storm went down to the kitchen. Deep down below her feet was a mysterious underworld full of secrecy and intrigue. She smiled. Putting rice on to cook, Storm went to the lower cellar and looked behind the Keeper of Keys, running her finger along the back of the painting, but it was too obvious a hiding place. The two sets of keys were accounted for. However, the large key to the locked door was no closer to being found. It was puzzling.

Chopping onion, mushrooms and garlic, she threw them into a pan with olive oil and chicken, adding a tikka masala ready-made sauce, some ginger, turmeric and seasoning. As the flavours cooked in, the scrumptious spicey smell of curry filled the kitchen.

Cooking calmed Storm and she enjoyed it, finding it therapeutic when stressed out or if she had a lot on her mind. She'd had plenty of practice, due to school anxiety, but also because she didn't want to eat jacket potatoes every night for dinner when her mum was working.

The dining room overlooked the bay, so they could still keep watch. Storm lit the fire and called Finn down from the Zen room. Adding poppadum, dips of mango chutney, Tzatziki and naan bread, she brought in dinner.

"Oh wow. You really are the best Storm."

"Helps me think."

"Eating?"

"No, cooking."

"Carry on thinking; that's all I say. This is heaven. Eating is what helps me."

After dinner, Storm gave Finn instructions how to clear up and sat with binoculars looking out across the bay.

"Empty any old food bits in the bin first." She called down.

"I know how to wash up. You just put them in the dishwasher. What a cheek."

"You have to wash the pot in the sink, Finn!" Storm laughed. "Have you ever actually cooked anything or washed up?"

"Erm yes! I've made a pot noodle, quite a few times!"

Storm put another log on the wood burner and settled on the window seat. She could hear Finn singing her favourite rock song in the kitchen, and the clatter of dishes. It was great having him around; he was such good company and slowly returning to his old self.

The weather was deteriorating rapidly, and the sky darkening ominously. Rain lashed against the window. The sea heaved as dark grey waves fringed with white raced inland, crashing onto the jagged black rocks, casting salt spray upwards . The lighthouse lamp flashed every thirty seconds warning ships to stay clear of the black sharp crag that lay hidden beneath. Not to be outdone in drama, the wind moaned in a ghostly manner whizzing around Puffin Island at a fast rate of knots. The sea mist typical of the area, called the haar, moved in like a giant cloud descending upon the earth.

The yacht appeared in the distance through the gloom.

"Finn! Finn!" Storm called frantically.

He shot up the stairs.

"They're back!"

"No way! In this." He said peering out of the window.

It was not a night to be out at sea.

Visibility was poor, but Finn and Storm could make out movement. The binoculars were powerful and they spotted hazy figures on the yacht. The next minute, a motorboat appeared. A second attempt perhaps at the afternoon's failed mission.

"Suicide in this." Finn muttered. "They must be desperate."

Storm looked at him but said nothing. It was not the time to point out that the weather had been just as bad when he journeyed from the boat house to the island, minus the sea mist.

"Just what I was thinking," Storm said. "If they're looking for something, why come out in this? Can't see much. It must be a drug deal or something."

"Yeah and there's like a time arranged for drop off and pick up. Unless they've already dropped off something, when we were underground on our way back from the rock pool earlier. We sat in the Emerald Pool Chamber for about thirty minutes, warming and having food," Finn pondered.

"The yacht moved off though, Finn. Remember? When we were still in the rock pool and there was no sight of anyone when we took the motorboat back over here?" Storm scratched her head.

"Wouldn't have had time."

"Who knows. Could be drugs or counterfeit money. Counterfeit's supposed to be big business at the mo," said Finn.

"Yeah, like you know that!" Storm said scornfully. "Maybe in some gangster movie on Netflix but not in Shelley."

"Rife in Edinburgh, Glasgow and London. My mate's dad dabbles."

"Sure he does, Finn."

Finn laughed. "Well my mate says he does. He's been inside apparently."

"Prison! How does he dabble?" Storm sat back.

"Washes counterfeit money through the restaurant he works at."

"Really! What, around here?"

Finn shrugged. "Apparently. He gets a percentage of the money he cleans. My mate says it's better when his dad's in the nick. Think he causes bother when he's home."

"Nice! He could be mixed up in this?" asked Storm. "Shall we head out?"

"No clue. But maybe." Finn pulled on a thick black hoodie. "Yeah let's go."

"Two seconds." Storm shot upstairs to her bedroom and returned with some military face paint her dad had given her. "Take the shine off our faces, so they don't show up."

The mist was now dense. Storm and Finn crept out of the front door clicking it shut. They moved slowly, Finn holding on to the back of Storm's hoodie. They made their way to the small forest and then tiptoed to the top of the cliff where the Cave of Boulders was. Lying flat just beyond the edge, they peered through the murky haze and rain.

They could hear voices in the distance coming from the sea. One was speaking in English this time but with a thick foreign accent. The second voice had a Scottish accent and the third Southern

English.

"Just leave the boat here!" Foreign ordered.

"I can't see shit." Scottish moaned. "Water's freezing."

The sound of splashing as the men waded to shore.

"Flaming pea soup," Southern English said. The voices were getting closer but the figures were still hidden by swirls of fog.

"We stick to the plan. Drop the goods off now…gets picked up first light. It had to be tonight or it's off," said Foreign shortly. "You want that. Them to go elsewhere!" He added angrily.

Lights appeared. Finn and Storm moved back an inch from the edge.

"What you on about? Nah, who said that. After all the work I've done. Let's just get a move on," Southern English snapped.

"English dude sounds like John the Psycho," whispered Finn into Storm's ear.

The wind whistled eerily.

"The accent maybe," Storm whispered back.

"Ahhh. Sake!" Scottish swore as he slipped on the rocks. "What you going on aboot all the work you done? Sat on your arse down south!"

"That was to take the heat off, in case the old bill was cottoning on. We wouldn't be here if it weren't for me. I found this place. It's thanks to me. Even shacked up with that loony bird to case this place, proper like; an' her little shit of a son!" Southern English sounded angry. "We've made a shit-load of dosh already under their noses, so some respect!"

Finn tensed. Storm instinctively put her hand on his hoodie.

"I bloody knew it," Finn hissed to Storm. "It is John the Psycho. What the actual hell!"

"Don't let them hear us," whispered Storm. Events had taken a dangerous turn for the worse. They were massively out of their depth. These men were serious criminals.

"Stop you bitching!" snapped Foreign.

Three dark figures dressed in black with woollen hats appeared through the sea fog, labouring up the beach. Southern English, who Finn had identified as John the Psycho, was carrying a black holdall. Reaching the Cave of Boulders, loud thuds sounded, as Scottish hurled rocks onto the sand. Storm and Finn were on the clifftop directly above. They slid backward further, barely daring to breath, praying the men wouldn't see them.

Rocks clattered, and scrambling through the hole, the three men disappeared into the cave. Moments later they re-emerged.

"We pick up the next batch tomorrow at noon and collect our percentage. Ahhh…" Foreign swore as he too slipped and fell on the sharp rocks, landing on his back. "Cut my hand..!" He swore again. Torrential rain cascaded. The wind howled at gale force.

"Five hundred thousand next haul. Lots of work to do. Gonna make a packet," Psycho John shouted over the din, as Foreign staggered, finally managing to stand up.

"Be able to treat your Mrs won't ya!" Scottish said spitefully.

"Gone," John the Psycho swore. "Packed up and cleared off. Took enough to get rid. I was gonna finish her. Happen I would have enjoyed it. Had it all planned."

"Aye, you like your plans," Scottish said sarcastically.

"Don't you two ever shut up! Like, how you say, an old married couple bitching. Put rock back and let's get out of here. Place gives me creeps." Foreign snapped limping down the beach.

Storm and Finn flattened themselves further into the grass. Finn was shaking. White spray foamed as the sea surged up over the beach soaking the men. Scottish was swept off his feet and swore loudly.

"So much for your perfect place, you numpty. Island's a death trap!"

The men squabbled all the way back to the motorboat. Finn and Storm crawled forward. They could just see the back of the men with their flickering lights as they searched for the boat through the thick white blanket of fog.

"Where the…?" Scottish was floundering in the shallows trying to locate the motorboat.

"Ere!" yelled John the Psycho.

The beams disappeared into the gloomy night. The wind was deafening.

"You ok, Finn?" Storm whispered.

Finn was almost vibrating with suppressed rage. "He was gonna kill my mum. I just wanna go down there and rip him apart…!"

"I know. I can't like even process it. He's totally satanic!" She shook her head. "Total psychopath!"

A loud cracking carried on the gale.

"Did you hear that?" Storm whispered.

"What?"

"Dunno it was weird…like a splintering noise."

"Nah can't hear a bloody thing in this."

"Shall we head in?" Hearing John the Psycho proudly declaring his plan to kill her aunt had shaken Storm. If Finn hadn't run away from Gravestone he and his Mother could both be dead. John the Psycho had made a declaration, not a threat. It was terrifying to hear.

Finn put his hand on her arm. "You wait here a sec Storm. I'm going down. Then we'll head back."

"Finn no!" Storm pleaded. "You can't mess about with these people. They're like lunatics. They'll hurt you."

"There's no one here to hurt me!"

"You're not taking it are you? Look at the weather they came out in. It is obviously massively important. If you take it you'll be dead. They'll hunt you. I saw it on a film the other day. This guy nicked drug money, and this gang found him, took it and killed him."

"They won't even know it was us. Plus we don't even know what 'it' is yet!"

"This is bad, Finn."

"Shh Storm! Stop stressing! I promise I won't nick whatever it is. Just wanna have a look. I need to do something after hearing what I just did. I'm raging!"

"Just be careful." Water ran down Storm's face. Her teeth were chattering. Finn and Storm were both soaked, filthy and frozen.

"Believe me, I'll be careful," Finn said, full of determination.

On his belly, he crawled down to the lower part of the cliff with an access point to the beach. Storm couldn't bear to watch and so she crawled after him. Just as they were about to climb down to the sand, there was a dark rapid movement in the distance near the location of the Rock Pool. Finn and Storm froze and flattened down.

A tall black figure, carrying a large bag, sped through the darkness towards the Cave of Boulders, his feet splashing through the high tide. Hastily removing the boulders with ease, he disappeared into the cave. Moments later he re-emerged, his dark bag bulging, replacing the rocks in a meticulous manner.

Finn made a jerky movement, his mouth opening to shout. Storm grabbed his arm, slapping her hand firmly over his mouth.

"Stay down, you lunatic," she hissed.

They froze as the figure stopped stock still like a cat, staring in their direction through the mist. Water wrapped around his ankles and the wind tugged at the balaclava that hid his identity. For a moment the man hesitated and took a step forward before turning and running at top speed to the end of the beach, where he disappearing into the haar.

"What the actual hell, Finn!" Storm whispered angrily. "Have you completely lost it?"

"Storm didn't you see who that was?"

"Errr. No. I can't see anything due to my eyeballs drowning in rain and fog."

"It was my dad! I think I know my own father!" he yelled, turning on Storm in anger.

"You're like obsessed. I'm quite worried about you to be honest. Finn, why would your dad appear out of nowhere in the middle of a storm, steal drugs or whatever it is, and then disappear again."

"I have no clue. I just know. And now we won't ever know what 'it' is 'cause my dad or 'the man' has just nicked it. So if we hadn't spent so much time arguing about it, I could have lifted it first."

"Yeah, and then had the cat burglar after us as well as the psycho gang. This is getting out of hand."

"Cat burglar," Finn smiled. "You always have to name everything, don't you."

"You're like mood swing a second, Finn."

A branch from the small forest on the island cracked and fell to the earth with a thud. Storm and Finn both visibly jumped.

"Maybe that's the weird noise I heard." said Storm. "Anyway how do you know that guy, whoever he is, wasn't the intended person to collect 'whatever it is'. He might be."

"Nah. Remember one of the gang said it would be picked up at first light by whoever and they'd be leaving another stash and cut of the money. I bet if we spy tomorrow we'll see the other gang turn up and be raging," Finn said confidently.

"Yeah, we should do that."

Finn nodded. "I'm going to have a scout. You coming?"

Storm nodded. "It is literally impossible to get any wetter. If we die of hyperthermia, it's on you."

Clambering down to the beach, they made their way cautiously. Visibility was so poor they could barely see in front of them.

"It's surreal. Feel as though I'm moving through a cloud," mused Storm. "If it's like vapour; it's weird how it's thicker in some places more than others. Like the mist's thicker here than up on the clifftop."

Storm and Finn sploshed along the sand to the Cave of Boulders. Finn was deep in thought and didn't respond.

"If it was my dad, he'll have gone underground via the Rock Pool to his hideout behind the locked door."

Storm shook her head shouting over the elements.

"I'm not saying you're wrong. Finn; just don't want you getting messed up if it isn't."

"Come on. Let's be quick before we die of cold."

Moving the boulders from the entrance, they shone the flash-light into the interior of the cave, expecting it to be empty. It was a small sandy space, dry and sheltered from the wind. Inside was a stack of plastic crates full of rope, tape and clear polythene bags. There was a mark in the sand where the black holdall had been placed, and a flurry of footprints. Finn immediately took a photo which would be no doubt scrutinised later for size and tread matching his father's.

Replacing the boulders, Storm took a branch with leaves and erased any tracks at the base of the cliff. At the cliff top she messed up the flattened grass and they retreated back to the Light House.

Shoving their soaking clothes in the washing machine, they changed into dry joggers and hoodies and sat in front of the fire in the Zen room drinking hot chocolate and munching crackers and cheese with grapes and crisps.

"I never knew it was possible to be so cold. Beginning to feel part of my big toe again." said Finn.

Storm checked her phone.

"Pop's op went well and they're defo staying at a hotel cause of the weather." She texted back. "All good. Glad it went well."

"Good news," said Finn, nodding and emptying the remainder of the crisps into a bowl.

"You were so sure it was your dad, Finn." Storm broached the subject that was bothering her.

"I am sure." Finn yawned. "I just know. Can we just not talk about this right now? I'm just enjoying being warm again and mulling over my first death threat, well my mum's really but maybe mine too."

"Scared you?"

"Nah I could 'ave 'im." He mimicked John the Psycho's southern English accent. "Proud I cracked him one, back in Gravestone though. Was a whopper. Course I didn't realise I was taking on a gangster!"

Storm laughed and hit him with a cushion.

Taking sporadic glances out of the window, darkness prevailed over the bay and there was nothing more to see. Tiredness overcame them, and drowsy from the hot chocolate and heat of the fire, they slept.

CHAPTER 17

Destruction

Sunlight beamed through the glass windows, waking Storm. It was 5am and the sky was a clear blue. The ocean, an innocent indigo, was still and calm. Marmite kneaded her stomach, digging in his claws and purring loudly.

Looking out the window, she picked up Marmite, stroking him. Rumbling, he butted her with his black head. The yacht was still anchored out in the bay. But the elegant vessel was no longer alone. Dumping Marmite on the ground, she grabbed the binoculars.

"Finn!" she called sharply.

"What is it?" Finn sat up as Marmite shot out the door, hissing at Marmalade as he passed.

"The Coastguard's out and a police boat. There's debris in the water and…." She moved the binoculars in the direction of the yacht. "No sign of life on the yacht."

Finn stood up stretching.

"Coastguard are out? Let's go!"

They grabbed their jackets, ignoring the protesting cats, and shot out the door in the direction of the forest.

In contrast to the blinding confusion of the night, visibility was excellent. The weather was warm and crisp. Storm and Finn ran from the forest to the place of surveillance they'd occupied the night before. Large black panels and splinters of wood were scattered all over the beach along with the mangled metal of the engine.

"The motor-boat!" exclaimed Finn.

Storm trembled as she viewed the remnants of the motorboat. A tall man with red hair wearing a coastguard uniform was standing on the beach taking photos of the destroyed boat and surrounding rocks.

"Charlie Golf this is Whisky 35 over," he spoke into his radio.

The radio crackled in response, confirming that three men had been fished from the sea in the early hours of the morning. Finn and Storm held their breath trying to hear further information.

"Can't believe we slept through something so important," Finn declared through gritted teeth. "Coastguards out in the night and we bloody missed it!"

"It must have been John the Psycho and his gang! It was like insane weather last night. They never made it back to the yacht. Must've been smashed to pieces on the rocks."

The red haired man's radio crackled.

"Three fatalities," The coastguard said. "Repeat: no survivors….Roger that….Out." He hooked his radio back onto his uniform.

"Oh my God, Finn. John the Psycho is dead!" exclaimed Storm.

"Talk about poetic justice. That's like karma, when someone gets what they deserve."

"I'm not a total idiot, Finn!" Storm shook her head. "I know what poetic justice is. I can't stop shaking."

"Same. It's all totally bizarre."

The coastguard vessel returned to pick up Whisky 35.

"Anything further?" he shouted over the roar of the engine.

His colleague shook his head and made a cut throat sign with his fingers crossing his throat. The red-head waded up to the boat and climbed on board. The boat disappeared heading towards Shelley Coastguard Station.

It was confirmed. The gang, including John the Psycho, had drowned.

"Bloody hell!" said Finn.

"You don't think that cracking noise I heard last night, was their boat hitting the rocks, do you?"

Finn nodded gravely.

"Probably. 'Spect they were battered on the rocks and drowned in seconds. Plus it was super freezing and foggy. I wouldn't wish death on anyone, Storm, but it was their choice to come out in that weather, and John the Psycho was pure evil. Boasting that he planned my mum's death, as if it was nothing. Truth. Hope he rots in hell. Last laugh's on him." His face darkened with anger.

"I know. It's just macabre," Storm shivered.

"Could have been me the other night," said Finn looking ashamed. "What an idiot!"

"Well it wasn't, so move past it, Finn," said Storm impatiently.

Returning to the Light House, Storm took out a large frying pan. Bacon and sausages sizzled in the pan, and the hearty smell of cooked breakfast filled the air. Cracking eggs and buttering toast, she carried it into the dining room followed by Finn who had made the tea.

"We need to unlock the Locked Door," Finn announced.

"But how?" questioned Storm frustratedly.

"Let's presume that the tall man in black: Cat Burglar, who appeared magically, is my dad, and he's hiding in the locked room for whatever reason. He came from the area of the Rock Pool. I think we should go see if anything has been moved underground, any trace of him...tracks, like muddy foot-prints, that kinda thing."

"Oh my God!" exclaimed Storm as an idea came to her.

Finn put a fork full of bacon, egg, sausage and toast into his mouth, looking at Storm quizzically as he chewed.

"I watched this film the other night. This guy, he put this piece of cardboard in the door and it can only fall out if opened. We should do the same with the locked door with thread or something. That way we'll know if someone's in there."

Finn gave her the thumbs up as his mouth was full. Washing their breakfast down with tea, they cleared up and disappeared down into the tunnel.

Storm put a small amount of Blu-Tack at the bottom of the door and another onto the doorframe, sticking black thread to it. Making sure it was secure, the trap was set. Grabbing diving gear from the store room, they made their way into the Emerald Pool Chamber, shining the light on the floor and walls as they went to check for any signs of disturbance. There were none.

"Oh my God!" exclaimed Storm.

"What!" Finn turned in alarm.

"Just remembered about the candlestick and stone in the bucket!"

Finn laughed. "Only people on earth to forget about discovered treasure."

Storm laughed, "Just been so much going on."

They swam around the Emerald Pool and the Creepy Cave, but there was no sign of activity there either. Changing into dry clothes, they returned to the tunnel. The thread was still there, and they decided to check out the boathouse cabin as it was another exit and access point.

Upon reaching the iron rungs that led up to the cabin, Storm inserted the keys and clicked open the locks. She was about to lift the trap door when she heard a strange noise coming from above. They froze. It sounded like a loud banging. Slowly, Storm relocked the entrance. They dropped back down into the tunnel.

"There's somebody there!" she whispered.

"Banging around!" Finn said.

"Let's go disturb them. Take the boat over. They can't know about the tunnel."

They sprinted back along the tunnel, replaced the keys, then took the motorboat from the quay, zooming across the calm blue sea. Arriving at the boathouse cabin, there was no sign of life. Securing the boat, Storm unlocked the door.

"Bloody Hell!" Finn walked in. "They may still be here." He warned, holding out his arm to prevent Storm coming in.

Paintings were askew, sofa cushions had been knifed, and white stuffing was spilling out, drawers were open and contents thrown on the floor. Storm barged past him.

"Oh my God!" Storm was shocked.

What a horrible day it was turning into. Drowned gangsters, and the boathouse cabin had been trashed.

"This is bad." Finn said horrified.

Storm tried to phone her mother. There was no answer, and she left a voice message.

"Mum. We're at the boathouse cabin. It's been trashed. Not sure what to do. Some men drowned last night near the island. We think John the Psycho may be one of them. Can you call me?" She put her phone back in her pocket.

"The lock didn't look forced. How did they even get in." Storm looked around.

Finn pointed to the window that was smashed at the back of the kitchen.

"Guess we wait until we hear from Aunt Lily."

After about ten minutes her phone rang. It was her mother.

"Are you ok?"

"Yes we're fine. The place has been trashed, Mum."

"I've made some phone calls. It's all in hand. You and Finn go back to the island; we'll be back later today with Grandad Flint. What you were saying about John…well he left Gravestone the day after Finn went missing, apparently. But why do you think John was there? He does know the island, as he's been there a few times in the past with Molly. But any particular reason?"

"Finn and I heard something when we were out for a walk yesterday. There were these guys in a boat that came from this big white yacht that's been anchored out in the Forth. They landed on the island. We hid and watched them. Finn thought one of the men was John the Psycho as he recognised him. John was boasting to his mates that he'd planned to kill Aunt Molly." Storm took a deep breath. "It was horrible. Then this morning their boat was smashed up and we heard the coastguard saying they'd drowned. Weather was grim last night. Shouldn't we call the police?"

There was a long pause as her mother digested the information.

"Trust me; it'll be taken care of. Can't say any more. You know how it is. It'll take Pops' mind off his ankle anyway as he's bored and crabby."

"Ok. The back window's smashed, and it's a mess." Storm frowned.

"Clare's husband can fix it. I'll call him. They have keys. It's important that you go back to the island and stay there."

After the phone call, they locked up and took the boat back over to Puffin Island.

"You know how it is," repeated Storm despairingly. "What a weird family."

"Totally weird," Finn nodded in agreement. "Let's have a think about the locked door and go exploring."

They sat in the Zen room looking out to sea. The yacht sat sedately in the bay. There was no sign of activity.

"Maybe they're keeping a low profile after the coastguard's visit," pondered Storm.

"Yeah and they've like lost four men. Three that drowned, and the idiotic one who got crushed," Finn replied.

"What if they're gonna come here next?" Storm looked out through binoculars.

"They've already searched the boathouse cabin. So I don't know. The yacht's parked out there for all to see and already gained unwanted attention," Finn said. "Psycho John's gang drowning will have put the yacht on the police radar. John may have planned part of this, but the person in charge of whatever they're up to is on the yacht, you can bet. He won't want his operation being uncovered."

"They'd have seen our boat going back and forth and maybe thought the mysterious Cat Burglar guy was using it and he'd stashed the stolen 'whatever', in the boathouse cabin," Storm theorised.

"They're clueless and desperate in other words." Finn said. "They need that money to be collected by the other gang in order to get paid and get the next stash. Plus the other gang will think they've been mucked about."

Finn's phone buzzed.

"Oh wow!" He looked appalled.

"What!"

"My mate Tom's just messaged me. Matt, the one whose dad I said was dabbling in counterfeit and lives in Shelley, well Matt's dad died last night. Drowned just off Puffin Island whilst out 'fishing' with two mates. No survivors."

He showed Storm the text.

"Oh my God!" Storm was shocked. "He must have been the Scottish dude. Poor Matt though, if that's like…his dad."

"I know. Exactly! Sounds like it was defo counterfeit money then," said Finn. "I'm genuinely worried that my brain is going to burst with all this activity and info."

"Is Matt ok? But you did say, his dad was nasty and a bit of a loser?"

Finn nodded.

"Tom didn't say…but imagine he's gutted. Prob better off, but even so…still horrible for him. Know it sounds harsh, but the dude was majorly corrupt!"

"I know what you mean," said Storm. "Things are getting weirder by the second. Going back to the key for the locked door," she put her hair up into a bun on the top of her head, "the person in the room…whoever it is….has a key. Grandad Flint has one, probably on his person. There will be a spare. There has to be. One that only certain people know about, so they can access the room when they need to."

"So it's in the safe? In Pops' study?" Finn frowned. "Not more codes please!" He groaned clutching his head dramatically. "No more!"

Storm laughed and then exclaimed holding her hands up, "What if the safe isn't in Pops' study? What if this whole place, well the world below us, is an actual safe. If you think about it…! All the keys and locks and codes. It's a giant safe!" exclaimed Storm excitedly.

"Yes!" Finn slapped her hand, in a high five. "Let's do a search. We'll start in the tunnels and search every inch."

Their phones buzzed.

"Dinner's gonna be at six in the dining room. Mum's making a roast."

"Oh yum. I love Aunt Lily's roast dinners!" said Finn happily.

"I've never known anyone eat so much. You're like obsessed with food!" Storm laughed. "They're heading back soon. Just waiting for Grandad Flint's painkillers."

"That gives us a few hours to find the key. I feel like I've been up for about five years," Finn yawned.

"Cause we got up at stupid o'clock," Storm kicked him gently. "Come on, lazy."

CHAPTER 18
Anger and Secrets

They walked slowly along the underground passageways searching for loose rocks, crevasses, anything they may have missed. Reaching the storage rooms they methodically went through the chest of books, supply cupboard, military kit, everything.

"Storm!"

Storm ran out to where Finn was standing glaring at the locked door.

"The thread! It's no longer attached. I bloody knew it." Crouching down they examined the Blu-Tack where the thread had pulled away.

"Let's just be really careful," said Storm nervously glancing around her.

"I think he's gone," Finn said. "I reckon that drop-off business was something to do with him being here. Now he's gone."

"If so, it'll be to do with work. Official. Or a secret op. Hmmm...."

"What?" Finn frowned.

"Maybe...Okay, so it was your dad. He collected the money!"

"You think he's involved?"

"Your mum and Dad had an argument about his deliberate involvement with a gang. Remember you overheard it just before they split." Storm grabbed Finn's arm. "He was undercover. Maybe he set them up. Psycho John's gang and the yacht! That's what all this is about. Organised Crime!"

Finn nodded, but his face darkened.

"Nice of him to keep us worrying he's dead or being tortured! Missing in action in the hands of God knows who...." Finn grimaced. "You've no idea the dark shit I've imagined."

"It's seriously messed up." Storm nodded.

"Like I know it's his job. But what about his son and what about my Mother!"

"From the conversation I overheard...it makes sense now. He's worried about them getting hold of you. Us. You don't think your mum was undercover too?"

Finn laughed disparagingly.

"Nah. I wish. My Mother is innocent and a bit naïve. She's only ever been out with Dad. Wouldn't have seen John coming. But Dad would have. He would've known all about John the Psycho's involvement in counterfeit, organised crime and still left his only son rotting in Gravestone with a known gangster and psychopath."

"They would've had John the Psycho under surveillance, in truth...as a person of interest. So if a real shitstorm occurred, they'd have stepped in."

"Maybe, but they didn't notice me leaving Gravestone, did they, when I ran away back up here?" He shook his head. "Who knows. I just...it's a lot to get my head around. I really hope my dad has left cause the way I feel right now!"

"Just a heap of maybes anyway, Finn, at the moment. As you say... who knows?" Storm exhaled a long breath. "Cause my dad would have known too! Remember he said, he was planning to extract you and Aunt Molly, in the conversation I overheard with Pops. He must have known. So many secrets..."

They sat in a gloomy silence contemplating the many secrets that shrouded their lives.

Finn suddenly sprang to his feet.

"Let them get on with it," he shouted angrily. "I'm done with it! Sick of feeling sad! Totally done with dark demonic thoughts all the time!"

Storm nodded, scrambling to her feet.

"Same, Finn! Totally!"

"And majorly done with adults playing God with our lives. Storm, we have lives too! I know our dads have weird jobs but seriously! I can't even think about it, at the moment."

"I know. Feel quite angry too!"

"We get on with our own shit. Finding the seventh key is our mission," Finn said, calming down with renewed determination. He took a deep breath. "Left to search: - we have the Emerald Pool Chamber, Dome of Breath 1, Creepy Cave, Coded Archways and Dome of Breath 2 and Underwater Well. Then if that's a fail, we'll have to look in the Ghost Ship."

He glanced at his watch.

"Blimey, it's ten past five!"

"And we're gonna have to shower for dinner. Damn!" said Storm. Suddenly she stopped in her tracks. Finn banged in to her.

"What?"

"That's it!" she turned excitedly.

"What's it?" Finn asked impatiently. "Don't say you've had an epiphany right on dinner time!"

"The Key. I know where it is. Dome of Breath 2 in The Coded Archways. TREASURE ISLAND out ISLAND TREASURE in. An underwater swim-in safe within a giant underground one. One that houses two precious things. An entrance and exit and the key."

"Swim in." Finn chuckled but his eyes gleamed with excitement. "Is entrance and exit one thing? I suppose it is. Well I think you may have cracked it, Cuz. But we have zero time left to find out!"

"What if Mum's in the kitchen. We'll have to say we've been in the cellars."

Putting the keys back behind the Keeper of Keys, they could hear Lily setting the table in the dining room. They shot through the kitchen along the long hall way and up the spiral staircase. Showered and changed into fresh clothes, they arrived at the dining room at five minutes to six. Always five minutes before was one of the rules of a military family.

They hugged and chatted like a long lost family. Grandad Flint looked pale but full of smiles.

"Couldn't understand why the damned thing was so painful. Seems it was set wrong. It'll be okay now."

"Must be relieved Pops," said Finn.

Molly and Lily dished out roast chicken with crispy roast potatoes, carrots, broccoli and Yorkshire puddings with lashings of rich gravy. Red wine was poured and grape juice for Finn and Storm.

Storm smiled at her mother and aunt. Molly's eyes were red where she'd been crying but she seemed to be alright. She'd obviously heard the news about John the Psycho from her sister in law Lily.

"You two look almost like sisters," Storm commented. With their long blonde hair, large eyes and slim figures, they were similar in appearance; only Lily's features were softer and her eyes were olive whereas Molly's were dark blue.

Molly smiled. "We do get mistaken for sisters." She laughed.

After they'd finished eating, Lily cleared her throat. "Finn, I hope you'll be okay with this. Molly wants to spend a month on the Isle of Mull. There's a place there that has counsellors, a spa, peace and quiet, and just time to spend healing from bad experiences," said Lily. "She needs time to get over all the business with John."

"And I was wondering if you'd be okay staying here," said Molly, taking a sip of wine. "I thought you'd be better with someone your own age. Hope we can put Gravestone in the past and I'm sorry about everything I put you through. I just lost my way a bit..." she trailed off. "I should've put you first."

Finn stood up and went and hugged his mother. Returning to his seat, he nodded. "I'm cool with that."

"Furthermore," added Grandad Flint, "the outhouses are going to be converted into a home for Molly and Finn. The island is our family home, and I for one, after events of recent weeks, would feel happier if we're all safe and secure in the same place."

"Oh my God, I can't believe it!" Storm was so excited.

"A toast to new beginnings," said Grandad Flint. They clinked glasses. "And to absent friends." His eyes wandered to the two empty chairs, where Flint Jnr and Josh usually sat.

A strange whizzing whining noise came from far out in the bay where the yacht was anchored. Everyone turned to the picture window that looked out for miles across the sea. Suddenly there was an almighty blast... BOOM! BOOM! BOOM!...and the whole island shook as the yacht literally blew apart before their eyes. The explosion hurled an obliterated mass of wood, metal and the entire contents of the vessel up and outwards, cascading with a crash down onto the black waves. A thousand bonfires raged on the tide. Then all hell broke loose.

Grandad Flint whacked the panic alarm located on the wall near the fireplace that alerted the coast guard and emergency services to respond to a major incident out at sea or on the island. A loud wailing siren shrieked and the lighthouse lamp flashed in quick pulses of red for the second time that month.

"What the hell?" said Finn as his brain struggled to articulate what he'd just seen and heard.

Lily and Molly ran over to Finn and Storm.

"Must have been a fuel leak or something. Terrible!" said Lily, putting a soothing hand on Storm's shoulder.

"Unbelievable!" added Molly, looking out in shock over the bay. She was trembling from head to toe.

Finn and Storm looked at each other. Storm was also shaking. Finn put his arm around her. Pieces of burning white elegance were everywhere, orange flames battling with the icy waves, and clouds of black arid smoke suffocated the air.

"Everyone alright?" demanded Grandad Flint.

"Yes. We are." said Storm quietly.

"Awful business. Be back shortly."

Grandad Flint disappeared limping at haste into his study and could be heard on the phone to the emergency services giving out coordinates and an incident report. To add to the commotion, a yellow boat with COASTGUARD appeared zooming across the bay at top speed. Helicopter's circled, and police boats and medics arrived. The air was full of noise, flames, smoke and chaos.

Storm and Finn were dispatched upstairs to the Zen room, as Grandad Flint dealt with the situation.

"Oh my God, Finn!" said Storm. The blast and noise had shaken her.

"Well that's the end of the yacht then!" said Finn shaking his head disbelievingly.

"You don't think?" Storm looked at him. "That's what they meant by things being taken care of."

"Nah, that's ruthless," he said looking out at the remnants of the burning vessel. "Depends though. If they were threatening the family."

"We don't know the whole story. I can't even think about this," Storm said, shaking her head. "It's too much."

Wrapping herself in a fluffy blanket for comfort, she sat huddled in front of the wood burner cuddling a reluctant Marmalade.

"Be loving, Marmalade," she said as Marmalade struggled to free himself. "I thought cats were supposed to be empathetic."

Lily and Molly appeared with mugs of hot chocolate and they sat looking out to sea.

"What do you think happened?" asked Storm.

"Must have been a fuel leak I suppose, gas explosion or something as it was so violent, can't imagine to be honest. Are you two okay?" asked Lily.

"Bit shaken. That was some bang. Just a bit jumpy," said Storm.

"Well, let us know if you need anything. Need to make sure Grandad Flint isn't overdoing it. He's supposed to be having bed rest and now all of this." She gestured out to the activity in the bay. "He never does as he's told anyway but he has just had an operation."

Lily and Molly left, and Finn paced up and down.

"We still need to finish our mission. Despite this." He waved out the window. "We need to find the key. I'm not losing any sleep over any of them. Evil nasty people."

"Just feel exhausted and my nerves are dying after the last couple of days. I think I'm gonna go to bed even though it's nine."

"Yeah good plan. Let's get up at four am. It's pretty much light then and there'll be no one about," said Finn.

He disappeared down to the bathroom, returning after a while with the red ruby stone and candle holder. Polishing them on his hoodie, he handed Storm gleaming silver and the stone.

"Oh wow!" The stone glinted. It was the size of a quail egg. "You think it's...like a real ruby?" quizzed Storm.

"I actually think it's possible. And that candle holder must have been pretty top quality as it's come up a treat...bit tarnished in places, but not bad."

The silver candle holder that had been hidden in water for centuries was gleaming.

"It must have been protected by the coral. Finn! Who knows what else is down there. I know a lot of its maybe been discovered but...!"

"And out there," Finn pointed to the Firth of Forth.

They sat up for fifteen minutes watching the police divers and coastguard searching for survivors but there were none. Storm yawned loudly and Finn joined in.

"I'm gonna crawl into bed. Shattered."

"Been a mental day and we hardly slept last night."

"See you at four. I'll set an alarm."

Storm walked sleepily down the spiral staircase to her bedroom below. Placing the silver candle holder and ruby on her bedside table, she climbed into the warm softness of her bed and shut her eyes. Tomorrow they would see what was behind the thick oak "Locked Door". Storm was convinced they would find the key in the Coded Archways. Tomorrow would be another exciting day.

CHAPTER 19

The Locked Door

Finn and Storm crept through the chilly morning air down to the lower cellar. Taking the keys from behind the painting of Puffin Island they made their way down into the mystical world below.

Risking waking those sleeping, Storm had made a flask of hot chocolate and lit the wood burner in the Zen room for their return, for it was a crisp cold day and they would be submerged in water and underground for some time.

Reaching the locked door, they checked the thread from the trap they had reset. This time it was still intact.

"So we kit up and go straight to the Dome of Breath 2?" Finn said, heading into the storage room.

"Yeah. I'm pretty sure," said Storm confidently.

Opening the Emerald Pool Chamber, Storm lit candles and lanterns. The green water gleamed magically in the candlelight. Immersing themselves, they swam the length of the pool. Finn led the way through Underwater Archway 1 and Dome of Breath 1 and the short tunnel. He stopped abruptly, and Storm bashed into the back of him. Finn signalled to go back and they awkwardly managed to turn and swim back the other way.

Resurfacing in the Emerald Pool Chamber, Finn shook his head.

"There's something in the way!"

"We can't get in?" Storm asked impatiently.

"There's a boulder that wasn't there before. Blocking the way!"

"What do you mean?" she demanded.

"A big old rock in the way! Maybe the explosion caused a rockfall."

"Unlikely. Think of all the storms that have battered the island. Is there any way past it?"

"Not sure. Can possibly squeeze past it. It may have just been a loose rock that fell when the island shook with the blast. Hope there's no one lurking in there."

"If they are I hope they've got thermals on!" Storm shivered. "Let's scout it out."

"Yeah we need to move before we die."

"John the Psycho's gang and the rest of them from the yacht can't be in there anyway. They're all dead."

"Truth. Unless you're worried it's the ghost of a drowned sailor from the Ghost Ship who wants us to KEEP OUT!"

Storm and Finn laughed.

"Before we die of hyperthermia, let's do it." Said Storm.

"You don't think my dad put it there to warn us off before he left?"

"Finn, we don't even know he was behind the Locked Door for definite. You talk as if we knew he was there and now he's left."

"I just have a strong feeling about it. Can't explain, and I did shout and kick the door a few times. I just thought it might be a message."

Storm nodded.

"Message received. But even he's not strong enough to pick up a massive boulder and stick it in front of entrance to the Creepy Cave! Cold's messing with your brain."

"Let's go."

Diving down into the water, Storm led the way. Reaching the end of the short tunnel, a large black object loomed up in the torchlight. Slowing to examine it, she saw that at first glance it appeared to block the way, but shining the beam upwards, there was a big enough gap for them to swim through as the boulder lacked the height of the archway. Swimming to the top of the arch, Storm swam through and Finn followed, although he had to detach his small oxygen tank and torch from his belt in order to squeeze through. Clipping it back on, he shone the beam around the murky greenery and the Ghost Ship. Pointing up, they swam upwards.

The Creepy Cave looked as it had on their previous visit. Shining the light upwards however, there was now a ledge three quarters of the way up the wall where the rock fall had sealed the cave many years ago. The boulder had fallen from there plunking to where it now sat.

"Nothing sinister," Finn looked relieved.

"Right, come on."

Reaching the fabricated door, Finn punched: 1-25-12-8-26-2-25-12 the code for TREASURE into the key pad. A deep clunk and the door opened. The Dome of Breath 2 was a gap of about one meter between the two doors. The ceiling was the shape of a Dome. Shutting the door, they began searching every inch of the area. It was the ideal hiding place, protected by coded doors on both sides.

Storm shone the beam on the floor, digging through sand to the rock below, pressing and running her fingers over the walls. Finn who was tall, searched the upper walls and ceiling. Nothing. Shutting the door they punched in: 16-26-19-8-21-11 the code for ISLAND and the outer door opened into the Well and the Underwater Rock Pool. They searched extensively but still there was no sign of a hiding place.

Returning to Dome of Breath 2, Finn closed the outside door. Running his fingers around the code panel, he pulled. It was stuck fast. Turning to the other door he did the same. Pulling on the right side of the code panel, it opened on hinges to reveal a flat panel with four key holes in it. Elated, Storm handed Finn the key ring with the six keys to the entrance of the tunnel. The four small keys turned and clicked. The panel opened, and there inside on a hook hung the illusive seventh key to the Locked Door. It was large and heavy. Taking it from the hook, Finn closed the panels. He was so excited he was blowing streams of air bubbles into the water.

Squeezing past the fallen boulder, they swam back to the Emerald Pool Chamber and clambered out of the freezing water.

Finn held up the seventh key. "I can't believe it!"

"Me neither!" Storm gasped through chattering teeth.

Storm was shaking with cold. They dressed quickly into fleecy hoodies and gym pants and gulped down steaming hot chocolate to revive their chilled bodies.

Standing in front of the Locked Door, Finn held the key up while Storm brought a lantern and torch.

"The moment of truth is upon us!" He declared with relish. "I can't believe we have the seventh key! Finally! What if there's just an empty room or cave behind it?"

"Get on with it, Finn!" Laughed Storm.

With a shaking hand, he inserted the key to the door and turned the key anti-clockwise. It clicked loudly, and turning the handle, the door opened inwards with ease.

CHAPTER 20
Within the Wardrobe

There was a small room with a large wooden wardrobe and a green canvas camp bed placed by the left wall. Storm opened the wardrobe. It was empty. On the bed was a military issue sleeping bag. Finn walked over to it.

"Storm!"

On top of the sleeping bag were three items. Two playing cards: The Ace of Spades, the Jack of Spades and a wad of fifty pound notes about two inches thick. Shining the beam on it, Finn drew in a breath.

"It's from Dad! I bloody knew it! This is his way of telling me. He's the Ace. I'm the Jack. He's had to go but he's telling me he's alive!" Finn shouted excitedly. "I knew he was. I just knew." Crouching down he smelt the sleeping bag. "It even smells of him. His deodorant." Finn stood with his hands behind his head as the reality sank in.

"All those months of not knowing! Thinking I'd completely lost it." Tears began to roll down his face. "And then believing he was mixed up in all this. So near, but didn't bother making contact. I was just so miserable and angry!"

Storm hugged him and he closed his arms around her sobbing into her neck as the trauma and stress of the last year erupted in a massive torrent of emotion.

"He would've Finn. He just couldn't for whatever reason."

Finn nodded.

They sat on the camp bed. Storm viewed their surroundings. "You okay?"

Finn smiled, wiping his face with his sleeve.

"Yeah I am now." He picked up the wad of notes. Written on the top note was a message. "Love you son. Always got your back!" Finn pressed it to his chest.

"He must have heard us in the passageway." said Storm. "We made enough noise."

"And all my rants," he said, flicking through the money.

"Not a bad thing, Finn. They were justified."

"Must be fifty odd grand here."

"His way of looking after you."

Finn nodded, putting the cash and playing cards in the zipped up pocket of his hoodie.

"My head's totally blown apart," he said.

"I know. I'm just relieved beyond words to be honest. Do you want to go back or explore a bit?"

"Now you've lost it! Finally opened the Locked Door, and you think I might want to go back! Nah, no way! We can process this shit later."

Storm laughed. "Totally. To be honest, I'm thinking this room is like tiny. I know the caves are different shapes and sizes but I dunno."

"I thought that when we walked in." Finn stood up and shut and locked the door. "Just in case."

Storm nodded.

"Most cupboards are musty if unused. There's that old, stale smell. That…" she pointed at the wardrobe. "Doesn't smell of anything."

"So you think it's like the entrance to Narnia?" Finn asked seriously, with a twinkle in his eye.

Storm squealed. "Yes!"

"I know you have mental health issues, Storm but...!" Storm punched him on the arm in jest. "Ow...But have you gone completely mad?"

"Oh, very funny. Obviously I don't mean Narnia." She laughed excitedly rushing to the wardrobe and opening the doors. "But I reckon it's hiding something."

Finn joined her. Reaching into the large cupboard, he pressed the back.

"No machinery here to slide away a panel. But maybe it's basic."

There was a shelf above the hanging rail.

Finn lifted the shelf and removed it and the rail, revealing a round hole. Inserting his finger, he pulled at the wood. A thin panel of plywood, disguised as the thick oak back of the wardrobe, moved forward and he pulled it out.

Behind was a man-made metal door with another code locking number panel.

Finn raised his eyes to heaven. "Now this is getting a bit tired now! This code and key thing. Not another three weeks to work this one out. Pleeeeese!"

Storm laughed. "It's supposed to be a safe, designed to protect something valuable from being stolen and keep thieves out, Finn; it's not a game or reality TV treasure hunt."

"Thanks for telling me that, Storm. I actually thought it was." He grinned.

"ISLAND TREASURE? OR TREASURE ISLAND?"

"I think that as the island is hiding something within, it's ISLAND TREASURE!"

They punched in the code for ISLAND TREASURE.

The door clunked open, revealing a short tunnel. A light switch was situated on the wall next to a thick oak door at the end.

"You think that's a trap?" Finn eyed the switch suspiciously.

"We're not in a game of Tomb Raider, Finn. It's a light switch."

Storm flicked the switch down and opened the door.

They both gasped at the same time.

"Oh my God!" said Finn.

Storm was speechless.

The door opened outward. There was a large square shaped room built inside the cavern. The walls were made of a grey protective metal. It was a giant vault. The walls were lined with steel and contained drawers of various shapes and sizes. Safety deposit boxes!

Opening one, Storm picked up a diamond necklace with a large emerald dangling from it.

"There are no locks on the drawers!" Storm held up the jewellery in astonishment.

Another drawer contained ruby earrings. Putting the necklace back, she opened a larger drawer that contained a silver dinner service. Finn opened other drawers that contained silk rugs and curtains.

"Maybe because the place is pretty secure anyway. Keys, locks and codes, that we discovered by pure fluke!"

Another large draw contained a very old beautiful violin and bow. Finn waved at Storm.

"There's another door."

Opening it was like walking into a royal palace. Vast paintings of horses, wild seascapes, Puffin Island, and mountains in the Highlands hung from the walls. A long gleaming walnut dining table with matching purple cushioned chairs sat in the middle of the room on a plush gold rug. It was set with silver tableware and crystal glasses. A silver and crystal chandelier hung from the ceiling. The walls were dressed with a light yellow fabric wall paper.

"Lost treasure," whispered Storm. She ran her finger along the table. Just a small covering of dust.

"Maybe not 'the' lost treasure but certainly treasure," said Finn looking around in awe.

"Family treasure?" said Storm. "or Crown treasure, protected down here from thieves?"

"Hopefully the first one, means we're rich!" Finn exclaimed. "But that's something to find out for sure. Maybe the Navy did find it after all and housed it here, to be guarded by Special Forces or maybe Pops did."

"You know I always wondered about the software story. I mean I know Pops is clever but he's more of an action man, same as our dads."

"Intrepid explorer, treasure seeker type."

"Exactly."

"I feel like I'm dreaming."

"Same. It's unreal."

Finn was checking all the walls, tapping and pressing.

"I always wondered if there was an entrance from Grandad Flint's study down to the underworld below, but I guess that would leave all this open to another point of access."

"I thought that too. Really the keys behind the Keeper of Keys isn't that safe to protect all this. But then there's the codes, and it took us ages to find the key to the Locked Door, so I guess it's as safe as it can be."

"I wonder if the Ghost Ship belonged to our ancestors or maybe a wreck they discovered and looted. It could have contained all this. Puffin Island is a prime location for treasure hunting," said Finn in wonder.

"Could well be. I just can't absorb all this!" said Storm.

Finn glanced at his watch. "It's eight fifteen!"

"We better go back."

Closing the door to the luxurious dining room, they made their way back through the vault, securing rooms as they left them. Turning off the light, they went back down the short tunnel through the wardrobe. Closing the thick metal door; the locks clunked, sealing the wealth and secrets within.

Finn replaced the back panel to the wardrobe and the shelf and they locked the Locked Door.

"I'm exhausted." said Finn. "Totally drained."

They still had to return the key to the Dome of Breath 2 door panel.

Putting on the cold, damp diving gear, they sank reluctantly into the freezing green water and swam to the Fallen Boulder. Squeezing past, they swam through the depth of the Creepy Cave, returning the key to its hiding place. Swimming back to the Emerald Pool Chamber, Storm rubbed her hair dry.

"You know, Finn, I felt differently when we swam back with the key through the Creepy Cave. It's like the Ghost Ship is now a friend, and all of this under the island is part of us now, and not some weird creepy discovery. And finding out about your dad, Uncle Josh being okay, is such a relief."

"I know. I felt the same. Kinda at one with it and not freaked out by it anymore. And knowing Dad's alive for sure. I feel ecstatic, can't describe it."

"Our treasure, or the Crown's, it's still unbelievable! I know what I want to do when I leave school or should I say when I leave homeschool!"

"Search for treasure!"

"Yes, totally," Storm laughed. "Can't believe how things have turned out, Finn. It's like everything's finally gonna be okay!"

"I know. We'll both be living here. I still can't believe it." Finn's stomach growled with hunger. "I'm so with you on the treasure hunting career. We'll do it together!"

Returning the keys to the Keeper of Keys, they showered and returned to the dining room for breakfast and then lessons.

After scrambled egg, bacon and toast washed down with tea, they sat with pens poised for the lesson.

"How are you both after yesterday's drama in the bay?" asked Grandad Flint, limping into the dining room.

"Good yeah." They replied.

"How's your ankle, Pops?"

"Better. Much better. Hardly feel a thing. How did you get on with *Treasure Island*."

"It's fantastic," said Finn. "Seemed so real like we were there. Didn't you think so, Storm?"

"Totally! Awesome! It was like we were there on the island."

"Excellent," said Grandad Flint his eyes twinkling. "I thought you would appreciate it."

"Now for today's creative writing class. I would like you both to write a short story imagining that you are treasure seekers who discover sunken treasure or come across a ship-wreck on a dark and stormy night. Just let your imagination go. Concentrate on plot, characters, pace and description. I've just got a few calls to make. Hand it in tomorrow and make it exciting! You can finish at noon today."

After he left Storm and Finn looked at each other and burst out laughing.

"He's like obsessed," said Storm grinning. "I think our answer to the question of who the treasure belongs to may be in today's creative writing assignment!"

"Oh my God, yes!" exclaimed Finn. "Must be in the blood though!" Finn smiled. "What a couple of weeks of adventure we've had!"

"Yeah, for sure. Move over for Locke and Swift, the new generation of Intrepid Adventurers and Treasure Hunters! Bring it on!"

The End

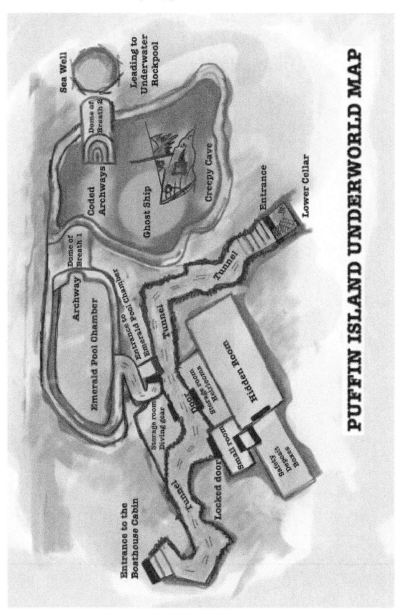

The 2nd in the Storm Swift Adventure Series:

Storm Swift
Missing in Action
Out soon...!

AFTERWORD

To all those suffering from Anxiety Disorder and other mental health issues: you are not alone, you are heard and understood.

Never give up the fight!

Stay strong.

ACKNOWLEDGEMENT

Thank you to my lovely Mother for her input, encouragement and for believing in me.

Thanks also to Aunty Dana for her assistance.

To my lovely children Tara and Krystian, who are talents in their own right.

Thanks to all the readers. I hope that you enjoy the Storm Swift books.

Printed in Great Britain
by Amazon

18931792R00081